Publications Presents...

A Novel by

AMANDA LEE

5 Star Publications
3383 Donnell Drive
Forestville, MD 20747

Deranged

ISBN -13: 978-0983247319
ISBN-10: 0983247315
Library of Congress Control Number: 2011928363
First Printing: July 2011

Printed in the United States

www.icon5star.com
www.tljbookstore.com
www.facebook.com/authoramandalee
www.authoramandalee.weebly.com

Dedication

I want to dedicate this book to my children: Ty'Shirra, Jamarious, Keairra, & Aunastazzia. I want to thank you all for being by my side through the good & bad times. Mostly my pissed off moments.

Love You ALL so dearly,

Mommy.

The Beginning

The day Nikki and I joined together as one was when Marvin Jackson broke my heart and pissed in my face. His motto was, "fuck one bitch today, and fuck many more the next day." I knew he was a dog when we first met, but I fell in love with him. I always seemed to get the men that didn't give a fuck about me. Men that used me for my pussy and money. *If they only knew....*

"Bitch, I told you that I don't want your sorry ass!" Marvin screamed.

"Please baby, I will do whatever it takes for us to be together. Don't leave me, just tell me what I have to do for you to love me," I begged.

"Bitch, stop begging. You sound like a fucking dog whimpering."

"Baby, don't leave me. Please baby, please. We can work things out. Deep in my heart, I'm suffering knowing that you are leaving me."

Marvin just looked down at me. He pushed me to the floor and demanded that I take off my pants. "Well bitch, let's fuck one more time before I leave your stupid ass."

"Yes baby, whatever you want me to do," I said as I looked at him.

I took off my pants and panties. He stood over me with his pants around his ankles while stroking his dick. I spread my legs, welcoming him to do as he pleased. Marvin got on the floor and rushed me like a mad man. He banged and banged until I screamed out for him. I loved that thug passion. You could hear his dick slapping against my pussy.

After he got off, he rolled over and said, "Bitch, I'm still leaving. Your pussy is good, but I found something better."

"You're sleeping with someone else?" I asked.

"Are you stupid? I've been fucking bitches ever since we got together," he boasted.

"For three years, there have been other women? How many?" I demanded to know.

"Bitch, I don't know. I use to fuck those whores, then come home and let you suck my dick. You seemed to suck it better when you tasted another bitch's pussy," he replied.

Something rushed through my body; I felt hurt, pain, and so much damn anger. I wanted to kill this pussy ass coward for making me feel like a two dollar whore. Marvin jumped up and pulled up his pants. "I tried to tell you before that I was fucking other bitches," he continued.

"When Marvin?" I asked.

"When I made a mistake and gave you gonorrhea. I wasn't trying to fuck that bitch raw, but her pussy was so good, I had to hit it raw," he smiled.

"You no good mutha-fucker!" I exclaimed.

"What bitch?!" Marvin yelled as he placed his foot on my neck while I continued to lie on the floor. "Fuck you bitch; don't you ever address me like that again," he continued.

He looked down at me and began pissing all over my face. I tried to get up, but he pushed harder on my neck with his foot. After he was done, he released me.

I jumped up and ran to the bathroom. He yelled, "Run and cry bitch; that's all you good for—crying and sucking dick."

I slammed the bathroom door behind me, ran up to the mirror, turned the faucet on, and began throwing water on my face. Although water dripped from my face, all I could see was fire in my eyes. Something was taking over my body, and for the first time I felt like killing his stupid ass. I'd done nothing but be nice to that fool and he was treating me like I was nobody. Well, I am somebody.

My face turned very cold, my heart began to beat faster and faster, and the palms of my hands began to sweat. I began swinging into mid-air like a wild woman. Rage began to take over my body, and the sad part about it was, I liked it. My heart was broken, and Marvin had to die. There was no way I was letting this pussy ass nigga slide with fucking over me and pissing in my face.

I stopped swinging in mid-air and just looked at myself in the mirror. I looked stupid crying over someone who didn't love me.

III

So now he'd leave without a sound, except for my shattering heart. Once upon a time, he was falling in love with me; but now I'm falling apart. He hadn't loved me for years, but that was okay; I had something for his ass.

"I know you not going to let that nigga use you and then piss in your fucking face," Nikki said.

"What can I do? He's stronger than me. Plus I don't want to hurt him. I love him," I replied.

"You love him? Love has you blind. Bitch, this nigga just took out his dick and pissed on you like you weren't shit. That's okay though. I will protect you like I promised," Nikki stated.

"You won't hurt him, will you?" I asked.

"Hurt him? I'm going to kill that bitch," Nikki replied.

"Nikki, no!" I protested.

"Just relax and let me handle this situation. You acting all scared and shit. I got you," she said.

After all the crying, my heart became so cold. Nikki had taken over, and I couldn't control her. At the moment, I didn't want to control her. I walked out of the bathroom slowly, feeling broken down and misused. I walked over to my bed, and pulled out two cold steel knives. This bitch nigga had to die; I carefully put the knives behind my back and walked slowly out of the bedroom door and down the hallway to the kitchen. Just as I thought, he was sitting at the kitchen table counting his money. Marvin had stacks and stacks of cash lined up. Fuck him.

"Bitch, are you finished crying yet? Because I don't have all night to be fucking off with you. I have this girl named Christy from down the street blowing me up, talking about she's ready to suck my dick," he said while laughing out loud.

"I don't want to give you up, but it seems like you are eager to go," I replied.

"Bitch, I don't want you. Never have and never will want you. I just wanted some of that good pussy you carrying around in those thongs; you had me addicted at one time," he replied.

"What happened to us?" I asked Marvin.

"Well, I found another bitch that had that good pussy like yours," he spoke as he turned around to face me.

"Did you ever love me?" I asked.

"No Nicole, I never loved you; but why would a nigga leave when you have your own house, car, no kids, and you give me all your money? Then on top of all that, you have some bomb ass pussy? I would be a fool," he replied.

"I would have given you all that anyway. You didn't have to pretend you loved me," I said.

"Shit, I had to get more out of you. If I hadn't pretended, you wouldn't have given me as much as you did. Bitch, you bought me a brand new Cadillac Escalade. I wouldn't have gotten that," he countered.

"I can't believe that you used me," I spoke softly.

"Believe it bitch," he replied as he turned back around toward his money.

I walked up to him as he held his head down, counting money. Before he could turn around and say anything else, I stabbed that bitch in the right side of his neck. Then I stabbed him again on the left side of his neck with the other knife. His whole body froze stiff; I began pushing the knives together, deeper into his neck. Blood spurted out as I tried to take his head off by pushing even deeper. He reached out as if he was going for his Glock .45 sitting on the table. I released the knives, and grabbed the gun; his body went limp.

I pushed the chair to the floor, and his body fell helplessly. He laid there shaking like the weak bitch he was, and we made eye contact. I stared into his eyes, trying to see the love, but his heart was so cold. I bent down and pulled my knives forward, slicing open his neck. Blood began to spurt everywhere as he placed his hands over the wound. I placed the knives on the table, and ratcheted his gun back, to put a bullet in the chamber.

"Nicole, please baby help me," he spoke slowly.

"Did you help me when you were fucking all those bitches behind my back, or beating me or breaking my fucking heart?" I replied.

"Please," he begged.

"Well, it seems like you're begging, bitch. Are those your words you repeated to me over and over again? It was bitch this and bitch that. Damn Marvin, I thought you forgot my fucking name," I spoke callously.

He lay on the floor gasping for air; blood was running down both corners of his mouth. I pointed the gun as he continued to stare up at me. I aimed it at his legs and released two bullets; one in each leg. "This is for all the pussy niggas around the world fucking over women and using them," I said. Two more bullets poured into his fat ass stomach, "This is for all the pain and hurt you put into my heart," I continued. Two more bullets violated his body; straight into his chest. "This is because I loved you unconditionally," I concluded.

His body slowly relaxed as blood continued to ooze out of his mouth and other parts of his body. I looked at him with no remorse; it actually felt good to release all of that anger and hurt. As his body lay there, I had a flashback of when he'd pissed in my face earlier. I slowly pulled off my pants and thongs and then bent down over his face. I grabbed his face, opened his mouth, and I pissed in it. As I pissed on his face, his mouth filled up and a mixture of piss and blood began rolling out of the corner of his mouth. I wanted to defecate in his mouth, but I decided that was too good for his no good, pussy ass. His eyes were open, looking towards the ceiling. I sat down on the floor, and just stared at him, as I held the gun in my hand; I threw the gun to the side on the floor.

"See Nicole, I've been trying to get you angry for a long time. Does it feel good to hurt him like he has done you all these years?" Nikki asked.

"It does feel good, but I no longer have him in my life," I replied.

"Fuck him. All you need is me in your life; and never forget, I'm the only one who loves you," Nikki said.

"I love you too Nikki," I responded.

"Let's get out of here before we get busted," Nikki urged.

I put my hands down on the floor and slightly lifted my body. I kicked Marvin's face to the left, and ripped his neck some more. It was already halfway hanging, but I didn't give a fuck. You could hear the skin tear as more blood oozed out.

"Fuck you; you fucking coward," I spoke to his body. "Who's the bitch now, Marvin? Pussy ass nigga!" Something inside of me had taken control, and I couldn't stop it. It felt so good; so right.

I got up to walk out and thought about fingerprints; I didn't give a fuck about that. My fingerprints were all over the house anyway. This was my shit. It would look suspicious if I disappeared, but then again, maybe not. They might think that whoever killed him had kidnapped me. I seriously didn't give a damn if they knew it was me or not, because I was leaving Seattle anyway.

Before dealing with the humiliation from Marvin, I'd had so many men use me because of what I could do for them. I had given niggas my money, bought plenty of cars, bought one home for a man and gave one man access to my bank account. At the time, it seemed right; they all pretended like they loved me, but really didn't. Most of them wanted to fuck and move on. I guess you could say I was weak. Well, I was tired of being weak. After I killed Marvin, I walked away that same day and started my life over. From that day on, Nikki and I were as one...

Chapter 1

After leaving Washington, I decided to move to Las Vegas, and everything was working out good. I had found me a new home in Ruffle Berry Heights apartments, a new job at Lee Law firm, which is now Webb & Lee Law Firm, and found a new man by the name of Jeremy Bland. Things were starting to look up for me; for the first time in my life, I was happy. I didn't have any female friends to hang out with, but that was okay. Jeremy took up all that time. My sex life was off the chain.

This brought to mind a sweet memory when my family was happy. My father had taken us all down by the lake not far from the house. He, my mama, my older sister Vanessa, and I were together as a family. My mama laid out a blanket and pulled out the picnic basket; we were happy like the families on television. Vanessa and I had our differences, but got along together that day. Father had packed a few turkey sandwiches with plain Lay's potato chips, grapes, apples, and homemade sweet tea. It wasn't much, but we were together. That day we all laughed and laughed until our stomachs hurt, as my father told hundreds of jokes. It was the happiest day of my life.

However, good things always come to an end. After that beautiful day at Lake Honeybee, we headed home, and we all sat down on the porch and watched the sun set. It was so beautiful. Later on that night, Mama tucked me into bed.

"Good night sweetheart," she whispered.

"Good night Mama. I love you."

"I love you too baby," she replied as she closed the door behind her.

That was the last time I ever heard my mama say that she loved me. Some memories were good to keep sacred, and others tore me apart. Things were good until the day Nikki came back into my life.

It's been two years and I haven't seen or felt Nikki until today. She's taunting me, wanting to be released because of Jeremy Bland; another wild nigga on the loose. I've tried to be patient with him. We have been dating for about six months now, but he wants to only be friends. What kind of bullshit is that? I'm supposed to just turn my love off and on like a light switch? Or become friends from lovers in seconds? Me giving him my love was very sacred to me; he had a special place in my heart, and I'd give him the world if I had it in my hands. If only he knew how deeply I loved him. I thought he loved me, but he had to break my heart for me to know what true love really meant. This love we had was stronger than what Marvin and I had, but it didn't mean a fucking thing to him. Jeremy spent time with me, spent his money on me, and showed me how to love someone. All the hatred I had

in my heart had disappeared because of him. Then one day, he took it all away. Just like that. Fuck him; pussy ass nigga.

It all started when we first met at my neighbor's house. He was looking so cute with his caramel skin, low hair cut, and small well groomed mustache. Jeremy was dressed in Polo pants, shirt, and shoes from head to toe. As soon as I saw him, I began aching from below. The good part was he wanted me just as much as I wanted him. My neighbor Melissa introduced us; she said he was a good man looking for a good woman. From that day forward, we were always together, but more as best friends rather than lovers.

We hung out, partied, and fucked each other. It seemed impossible that he wanted to be just friends. We shared secrets with each other, and we loved each other unconditionally, I thought. I guess he wasn't feeling the same way as I.

"Nicole, you are a good person, but I think we should stay on the friend level," Jeremy said one day.

"Why? Did I do something wrong?" I questioned.

"No, I just see us as being best friends. You're just like one of the guys to me; and I love that shit," he continued.

"Well, I don't want to be friends. I want us to stay just like we are: together," I protested.

"Damn Nicole! My mama said you would make this hard for me," he blurted out.

"Your mama? What does she have to do with this? You're saying you don't want me?" I asked.

"I can't say I don't want you; I just don't want to be in a relationship with you anymore. To be honest, I love living the single life; hanging out with the fellows, fucking whoever I want," he stated.

"So, this is all about you fucking other women?" I asked.

"Yeah, it is. I want to be free," he admitted.

"Well, if you want to be free, then I have no choice but to let you go. Just be sure this is what you want, because I just might not take you back," I replied.

"I understand Nicole, and I'm sure. I still want us to hang out and fuck every once in a while, if that is okay with you," he stated.

"Let me get this right; you don't want to be in a relationship with me, but you want to hang out and fuck me whenever you feel like it." I said.

"Yes, that's basically it," Jeremy said.

"Did you ever love me?" I asked.

"To be honest, no I didn't. That's why I never told you I loved you. Those words are sacred to me, and I'm not going to say it unless I mean it," he replied.

"I see how you feel. I guess I was misunderstanding how you felt about me. We were together every day and you're telling me that you never loved me? Well, I guess I was a damn fool to believe that you would love me," I said.

4

"I didn't mean to lead you on, or pretend like I wanted a relationship with you. At the time, that's what I felt. Don't get me wrong; you have some fire-ass pussy, but I want to explore more," he replied with a very serious look on his face.

"I do understand that, but I refuse to let you go. We can be friends or whatever you want to be, but I will have you one day. I love you so much, that I'm willing to do whatever it takes to keep you in my life. If you want me to kill, then I will. It's whatever you want, but you will be in my life," I replied.

"Girl, stop talking crazy," he responded.

"I'm serious. Why would you say I'm talking crazy? I'm expressing how I feel about you," I stated.

"You're really scaring me right now. Nicole, you are talking crazy. I just want to be friends; maybe fuck every now and then, because the pussy is too good to let go. But girl, stop talking crazy," he replied seriously.

"I'm going to do everything in my power to make you mine. Just remember that. You say that you don't love me but you will love me one day. All those other women will never love you like I do. Friends are good, but just remember: that's what you want, not me. I will have you one way or another," I responded.

He just looked at me and walked out shaking his head. "You tripping," he said.

From that day on, I was like a mad crazy woman. I didn't want any bitch near Jeremy; he was going to be all mines. Either

he was going to be mine willingly, or I would force him. It didn't matter to me.

For months, I pretended like everything was alright. We still hung out, and every once in a while when he was drunk, we fucked. The only thing he was doing was keeping my dreams alive of us being married one day. Right now, I'm sitting outside his house because he took this woman named Lucy out on a date. Lucy is a thick dark skinned chick with a big ass. He has a thing for a pretty woman with an apple bottom ass. Her ass looked like it was sitting on her back. I don't see why he wanted to fuck with her. She would never compare to me; I looked so much better than her. She had a big fucking head and big lips, and her hair was short and nappy looking. This bitch looked like the type of ghetto ass female that he said he would never have as his wife, but here he is fucking one. He got this bitch straight up out the hood; a gold digger that will never satisfy him emotionally or make him happy. Why can't he open up his eyes and see I'm the right one for him? Then again, he is a fucking dog, and dogs will fuck anything moving. Still, I loved this dog and wanted him to be mine; I would definitely train him the right way. It would be my way or no way; life or death, whichever he preferred.

He would probably kill me if he knew I was stalking his ass, but I don't give a fuck. Where does he get off fucking other women and still wanting me? He wants to eat his cake and have it too, and right now, I will give him that. Later he will see that I'm the only woman he needs in his life, because I'll be so good to him that he won't even need his mother around.

Jeremy took his guest out on the balcony as they sipped on drinks. It began to piss me off royally when I heard her laughing.

He was probably telling her those stale ass jokes he used to tell me. Some were funny, and others he could have kept to himself. Her laugh was so beautiful, and it made me jealous, but her fucking teeth were crooked and needed braces. The moon glared down on her face as she laughed.

I sat there with my head down thinking about how Jeremy and I would get drunk and fuck all night. We would pop a roofie and just do the damn thang. One night when we came from a barbecue over at a friend's house, we went back to my apartment and continued to mix drinks. Jeremy stripped naked and walked around with his dick hanging. My pussy began to jump, ready for him to bang the fuck out of me. I sat out on the balcony with my vodka and orange juice in my hand, and he walked over to me and put his dick in my face. I sat my glass down and slowly began sucking him with no hands. He grabbed my hair with both hands and slowly guided me.

Jeremy moved back and reached out for my hand. I placed my hand in his and stood up to face him. He began kissing me passionately. I put my arms around his neck, and he put his arms between my legs and lifted me up in the air. I reached down and guided his dick into my pussy. He shoved it in and began ramming me. You couldn't hear nothing but dick and pussy slapping against each other. Jeremy walked with me inside to the bedroom.

As he put me down on the bed, he laid down beside me. I climbed on top of him and we got into the sixty-nine position. He licked and I sucked him until we both came. I continued to suck him and finally, he got up and fucked the hell out of me all night. He put his dick in every hole I had, but I didn't care because my

man loved me. We fucked so much that the next morning we were sore. That night played over and over in my head; I wanted it to be like that once more, and I would kill to have that in my life again.

"Hello. Earth to Nicole," someone said.

"What?" I jumped, looking for whoever had spoken.

"Get out the car and interrupt them," Nikki said, invading my mind.

"No, I want him to be happy," I replied.

"That's how Marvin fucked you over. By you being a dumb bitch," Nikki pointed out.

"No Nikki, go away," I replied while shaking my head from side to side.

"Get out bitch, and see what the hell they are doing. Have you noticed they have disappeared?" Nikki asked while opening the car door for me.

"I can't Nikki. I can't go up there. I don't want my heart broken," I said, while resisting the urge to get out.

"Bitch, you are already heartbroken. He told you that he don't want you. What more do you want? That nigga don't give a fuck about you. Get out," Nikki demanded.

I jumped out of the car with a stone faced expression on my face. As I eased up toward the balcony, I could hear Lucy moaning. My heart began to skip beats, and that rage entered my mind. I walked up close enough to see through the wooden balcony;

8

Jeremy had Lucy on his new Darryl Carter lawn chair with her legs folded back towards her head. That was the same chair where he'd fucked me for the first time. He was licking her pussy slowly like he use to do me. A tear started to fall from my face, but Nikki took control.

"Bitch, you better not cry," she demanded.

"Leave me alone Nikki," I said.

"I'm so fucking serious. Don't you start that damn crying!" Nikki repeated.

I didn't respond, and only shook my head as I continued to watch. Lucy sat up as he unbuttoned his pants, and pulled them down around his ankles. He then lifted his shirt over his neck and head. She began to take his cock into her mouth, and it seemed like they were moving in slow motion. Jeremy moaned until he couldn't take it any more. He motioned for Lucy to lie back on the lawn chair, and he entered her passionately. He began slowly, and then began to bang harder and harder. I could hear them so clearly; nothing but cock and pussy slapping against each other. He went into the slow rolling mode; stroking and stroking until he saw her cum on his cock. He loved that shit.

After a while, he flipped her over onto all fours, and took her doggy style. She seemed to cry out louder as he banged. I had to move closer to see; I really wanted to see the expression on his face. I moved closer to the balcony behind one of his bushes, and I was right there near them. They both were so deep into it, they wouldn't have noticed anything moving; no way.

"Damn girl, I'm about to nut. Come suck me," Jeremy gasped, as if he was almost out of breath.

Lucy jumped around and began sucking on his cock as hard as a vacuum cleaner sucking up trash. He moved her head back and busted all in her face, and she had her mouth open like a little dog, just licking it all up. I was looking into his face as his eyes were closed, and he had a frown on his face that I had never seen before. She must be damn good; I wanted to jump up and kill the both of them bitches.

"Go on and kill them. You know he's going to let her stay the night," Nikki kept repeating.

"Stop it," I whispered.

"Kill them. I'll protect you from him. Kill them!" Nikki pressed.

Jeremy and Lucy picked up their clothes, and went inside the house. I stood up as he closed the balcony door. If he'd looked harder he would have seen me. I was so hurt, but that was okay; he would get his.

I ran back to my car, while tears filled my eyes. I stumbled and fell to the ground; I laid there on the ground crying and feeling sorry for myself. I thought I would never feel this pain in my heart again.

"Get up, you stupid bitch," Nikki mouthed off.

"Leave me alone Nikki," I sobbed.

"You just saw this man fuck somebody else, and you're on the ground crying. Get real. Go kill that nigga," Nikki retorted.

"No, I refuse to hurt Jeremy," I said.

"Fuck Jeremy, he doesn't give a fuck about you," she spoke madly.

"No. No. No," I gritted my teeth and whispered, while beating the ground with my fist. There I was on the ground pounding away like a mad psycho, when suddenly I heard noises coming from the front entrance. I jumped up and ran behind another hedge bush. Jeremy was walking Lucy out to her car. He stood there next to her holding her ass in his hands. They stood there for a few minutes having a deep conversation, but I couldn't hear shit they were talking about because Nikki was talking in my ear.

"You're a sad bitch Nicole. This nigga hasn't even thought about you and you standing in his bushes feeling stupid," Nikki ranted.

"I'm not stupid," I protested.

"I'll be damned if you're not stupid. Bitch, you are pathetic," Nikki said.

I watched as they kissed passionately, then she got in the car. He watched as she drove off, then he stood there looking toward my car. There were many cars on the street, but he was looking directly toward mine.

Suddenly, his cell phone rang from inside the house. He looked toward the house, then back at my car. Then he ran toward the house to answer his phone. That was my chance to get away; I had begun to run towards the car when he rushed back outside. I hit the ground again to hide. He had the phone to his

ear talking to someone, and he sat down on the front steps just talking his ass off.

"See bitch, you on the ground crying and shit. Now this nigga is going to bust us," Nikki accused.

"He's just talking," I said.

"Look now. That nigga is walking towards the end of the driveway. I just pray that he doesn't know that's your car. You stupid bitch," Nikki mocked.

"Stop calling me that. I'm not stupid," I said.

"Yes you are stupid. We are about to get busted," Nikki said.

We both got quiet. Jeremy stood at the end of his driveway, talking and looking out at my car. He was about to cross the street, but was stopped by his next door neighbor Jim. They began talking and he walked over toward Jim's house. They began chatting like two old women catching up on old times. What the fuck? I could see that Jeremy was talking, but he was keeping an eye on my car. Jim looked out towards the street trying to see what Jeremy was staring at. I was thinking to myself that this nigga was going to head towards my car as soon as he got the chance. I would just fall dead right here behind the hedge if he went over there.

Finally, they stopped talking; Jim headed back towards his house and Jeremy walked back toward his door. He was probably glad Jim had shut his mouth, so he could go back home. He looked out at my car and went on in the house, and damn was I glad. My heart skipped beats; I was scared as hell. As soon as I saw the

coast was clear, I ran like no tomorrow. I ran like I was running a race out on the track field. I looked back at the house and saw the living room lights go out. I cranked my car and pulled off. Something told me that he would come back out to the street to see if that was my car leaving or not.

"Damn Nicole, you fucking around crying and shit; Lucy got away," Nikki complained.

"Leave me alone Nikki. Leave me alone!" I yelled as I jammed on brakes, stopping in the middle of the street. Nikki began to hit the stirring wheel, out of control. She busted the rear view mirror and damaged the dash board. Her right hand was bruised badly and bleeding because of all of the beating. She began to shake like she was going into shock.

Suddenly, the phone rang; it was Jeremy. I picked up the phone to answer, but Nikki threw it on the floor, busting it into pieces.

"Bitch, don't you dare answer that phone," Nikki said.

"Nikki, that was Jeremy," I replied.

"Get a grip. You are pathetic," she said.

"Nikki, that was Jeremy. He wanted to talk to me," I said while crying again.

"You make me sick," she spoke in a rage while stepping on the gas pedal. The car began to race down the street going from 80 to 85, then 90 mph.

"Stop it Nikki. Stop it!" I yelled for my life.

13

"Die bitch, die! You don't deserve to live. Either you kill Jeremy, or I will!" Nikki screamed.

Those were the last words I heard before my car dived into a closed convenience store. Glass shards flew into my face, and I collapsed. *Kill Jeremy or I will* kept ringing in my head. What was Nikki going to do next? I couldn't control her anymore.

Chapter 2

"Nicole, wake up," a familiar voice spoke.

I woke up to look into the eyes of my sister Vanessa. She looked the same as two years ago; hadn't aged at all. I was so furious to see her there. Rage rang out, and Nikki was there.

"What the fuck are you doing here?" I nastily asked.

"You had a car accident, and they found my number in your purse," she replied gently.

"Who the fuck is they? I don't want you here," I angrily responded.

"Nicole, I called your sister," Jeremy spoke up.

"Who the fuck asked you to call my sister, out of all people? I told you about her," I said while looking at her.

I turned around to see him standing there with his sorry ass mother, who was looking at me like I was a disease. Her expression made my anger worse.

"Everybody get the fuck out. I don't need anybody here," I spat out.

"Nicole, we just want to help," Vanessa replied.

"What did you call me?" Nikki said.

She looked at me, as if trying to look through me, "It's happening again,.." she said as her voice trailed off.

"Bitch, get out. If I have to tell you again, I will hurt you. I don't want you here," Nikki said.

Jeremy's mama spoke her mind. "Somebody stop that devil from cursing," she said.

I turned around and looked at her. "Why the fuck is you here? I don't even like you," I responded.

"You better watch your mouth. You don't know who you're talking to," she replied.

"I don't give a fuck. Get the fuck out!" I yelled.

Jeremy interrupted, "Girl, you need to calm the fuck down."

"Bitch, you and your nasty ass mama need to leave," I responded.

"Calm your ass down Nicole," Jeremy spoke as he walked up to me.

"Don't stop her son; I will whip her ass all over this hospital," his mama said.

"Old woman, you ain't going to do shit but get the fuck out of my room. I don't want you here, I don't want your son here, and I sure don't want that bitch over there in my room. *GET OUT!*" I yelled at the top of my lungs.

16

I jumped up off the bed and jerked all the wires from me. Beeping noises began going off, and the grip fell on the floor as blood started coming from my hand. "Stop it Nicole," Vanessa demanded.

"Stop calling me Nicole," Nikki yelled and rushed Vanessa. She began to fight her, and Vanessa fought back. Jeremy tried to separate them, but Nikki threw him back and loudly yelled, "Get off me!" Jeremy rushed back up to her, trying to hold her down. He and Vanessa were struggling trying to hold me down. Vanessa got pushed to the ground, and Jeremy and I went down to the floor fighting. He was holding my arms so tight to my body that I couldn't breathe.

"Calm down baby!" Jeremy yelled out.

"Let that devil go!" Jeremy's mom yelled at him.

"Get off me! Get off me!" Nikki continued to scream over and over.

"Nicole, please don't do this!" Jeremy begged.

Nikki began to yell louder and louder as the nurses rushed in to dope her up. A nurse grabbed her upper arm and stuck the needle in, pouring medicine into her body. Nikki fought for a second, then passed out. She was getting stronger and stronger. I couldn't fight her anymore. The truth be told, I didn't want to stop her, because it felt so damn good.

Hours later, I woke up to see Jeremy standing over me smiling. "You are awake," he said.

"Why are you still here? I thought I told you to leave," I said.

"We are best friends. I can't leave you up here by yourself. I don't want you to be alone," he replied.

"Where's Vanessa?" I asked.

"She and my mother stepped out into the waiting area. The doctor thought it would be best for them, since it made you so angry to see them here," he replied.

"The doctor was right. I hate my sister and your mother hates me. Why would I want all that negativity here? I'm having enough problems," I said.

"What happened to cause you to wreck your car?" Jeremy asked.

"I don't remember. Everything seems to be blank right now; just a blur," I replied.

"I thought I saw your car parked in front of my house last night. Was that you?" he asked.

"Why in the hell would I be parked outside of your house? You're not that important to me. What are you trying to say? I'm stalking you now?" I replied.

"I didn't say that. Can I ask a question without you getting all upset?" he asked.

"Hell no! Don't ask me a mutha-fucking thing!" I retorted.

"Calm down, why do you get so angry with me? I care about your stupid ass," he replied as he walked up to the bed and placed his hand on my arm.

"Well, I don't want you to care about me. You can get the fuck out too. I'm so fed up with all this shit with you," I responded.

"Fuck, Nicole; you might be stalking me. I don't know, and I don't give a fuck. I was worried about your stupid ass, because I fucking love you man," he said as he put his hand on his head. He looked at me and yelled, "Fuck!" and walked out of the hospital room.

I looked at him as he walked out. I turned over, and stared out the window. Fuck him.

Chapter 3

Weeks passed before I had another episode like that. My sister had left town the next day, after Nikki attacked her. However, we had an interesting conversation before she left and I was dismissed from the hospital.

"Nicole, you know I love you," Vanessa stated while sitting.

"Stop calling me that. My name is Nikki," I replied.

"I thought you did away with your imaginary friend," Vanessa said.

"She's real. You can believe that," I retorted.

"Whatever, Nicole. Nikki. Whoever the hell you are. I'm so tired of you trying to blame me for all that's happened to you," Vanessa shot back.

"Bitch, you are the reason why all of this is happening to me. Can't you see? All of this is because of you. You are the reason Nikki is in my life," I responded.

"Why?" Vanessa asked.

"You didn't protect me Vanessa. I'm your sister, you fucking bitch. You failed to protect me," I retorted.

"I know, but I have apologized a thousand times," Vanessa pointed out.

"Fuck you Vanessa. You will pay for all of this. You and your fake ass mama," I responded.

"She's our mother," Vanessa said.

"No; she's yours. Not mine," I protested.

Vanessa walked out that day, and didn't look back. I wanted her out of my life, because Nikki was my life now. Since it was beyond me, I couldn't stop it. Nikki was getting stronger and stronger, and there was not a damn thing I could do about it. After the accident, I had to get another car, and the insurance fixed the store I'd torn up. The insurance company gave me a check worth the value of my car but I had already paid it off, so I chose to just buy me a new Mercedes; so sweet. However, besides the new car, it seemed like my life was falling apart.

As I sat in my apartment, I heard a knock at the door. When I opened it, to my surprise it was Jeremy.

"Hey baby, I decided to come by and see if you needed any company," he joked while hugging me.

"Sure," I replied in a dry tone.

"Well damn, doesn't seem like you are happy about seeing me," he frowned.

"What do you want Jeremy?" I asked.

"Seriously, I came by to see if you were okay. I don't want to lose a good friend like you. You really scared me," he said.

"I apologize for that; now you can leave," I said with a little anger in my voice.

"Please Nicole, I just want to be near you, and make sure you are safe," he said softly.

"It makes me feel good to hear those words come out of your mouth," I replied.

"Anything for you; I'll always be your knight in shining armor," he assured me.

I didn't say a word, and just sat on the couch watching Law & Order. Jeremy sat down next to me, and I leaned in toward him; he opened his arms so I could lay my head on his shoulder. He gently placed a kiss on my forehead, and began stroking my hair. Tears began to form in my eyes, but I didn't let them fall; I knew that Nikki would take over and ruin my day if I did. So, I sat there patiently, and enjoyed the man that I loved so much. One day, he would learn to love me. All I had to do was do whatever he wanted me to do. If he wanted to sleep with other women, then I would stand by as he did so. I wanted to be a part of his life forever, and not just be so-called best friends, as he said. The good thing is, you have to be friends before you can become lovers; I've always believed that. We can learn more about each other, then become as one.

We must have fallen asleep, because I woke up and Jeremy was holding me in his arms as we lay on the couch. This was the way he used to hold me, and make love to me all night long. I felt

him move, and pretended like I was asleep. He sniffed my hair and held me tighter; it felt so good.

Suddenly, thoughts of him fucking that Lucy woman awhile back started rushing into my mind. I could still see him eating her nasty ass pussy, and now he was breathing on me like nothing had happened. I should have just killed him right then, but that would be impossible, because how would I explain it to the police? Fuck that, I'm not ready for jail. Nikki might go, but not me.

Other lovemaking thoughts came to mind as I pressed my ass up against his cock. That would surely get his attention. Jeremy began to moan in a low tone. I rolled my ass slowly until he was fully hard and ready. I turned around to face him, and we kissed passionately. He kissed me back like I was the only woman in the world he desired. I slid off the couch, unbuttoned his pants, and began pulling his boxers over his cock. It was standing at attention and ready to march.

"What you doing girl?" he asked softly.

"I'm about to give you head. What else?" I replied as I placed my mouth on his cock, making him moan louder.

"Damn girl, you sure know how to make a man happy," he said between moans.

"If you want me to stop I will," I teased.

"Please don't stop. Just keeping doing what you do best," he replied.

Those words stuck in my head, because Marvin used to say that. My mind flashed back to when Marvin stood over me and forced his dick down my throat. He came in one night and woke me up. He walked up to the bed, and he yelled for me to wake up. I woke up, looked up at this drunken fool, and saw that he had no clothes on. His dick was already hard and ready to fuck. As I wiped my eyes, Marvin slapped his dick across my cheek. He grabbed my hair and forced his dick in my mouth, wanting me to suck him. I did as he asked me, because if I'd refused he would have gotten mad and beat me. My mind told me to go ahead and kill that mutha-fucker for treating me that way, but I loved him too much.

Now as I gave Jeremy head, I heard a voice say, "Go ahead and kill this mutha-fucker like we did Marvin. Look up at him; his eyes are closed. He will never know what hit him. Pick up that lamp and knock that nigga the fuck out," Nikki spoke.

I stopped sucking him for a second, and shook my head from side to side.

"What's wrong with you?" Jeremy opened his eyes and asked, as he grabbed me by the chin and tilted my face up.

"Nothing," I answered, as I put my head back down and continued to suck.

"Kill this weak nigga Nicole. He's treating you just like Marvin. I will protect you from harm like always. Kill him," Nikki kept saying in my head. I stopped again and shook my head. As I looked up at Jeremy, I could tell he was wondering what was going on with me. I jumped up and began walking back and forth, shaking my head.

"What the fuck is wrong with you?" he asked.

"Stop talking to me. Stop fucking talking to me!" I yelled out.

"Baby, what's wrong with you. Did I say anything wrong?" he asked as he walked up to me and wrapped his arms around me gently.

My body became weak and I hugged him back. Nikki had to stop fucking with me. We killed Marvin and she wouldn't let me live it down. She had the taste for blood, not me. I would keep her secret, but would not kill for her. I love Jeremy and will not harm him. He continued to hold me for a few minutes, and then stood back and looked into my face. "Are you okay?" he asked.

"Yes, I'm okay baby. I apologize," I replied.

"Are you sure? You know I'm here to protect you," he said.

"I know Jeremy. I know," I replied back.

It made me feel so good to hear him say that. Once he sat back down on the couch, I got down on my knees again and began sucking him more passionately. I had to focus on something else besides Nikki. She was being a real bitch right now. I had worked too hard to get this man, and I wasn't about to mess it up just because she wanted to taste blood.

To change my thoughts, I imagined me being Lucy as she sucked him. Jeremy welcomed me to take his whole cock into my mouth, and he began to play with my pussy through my short pants. I took them off as I continued to suck him. Jeremy got up and lay on the floor as I sucked him, and he pulled my ass to him,

biting me. He lifted my leg over his face and began to attack my pussy wildly. Him sucking on my clit and biting my ass turned me on so much, as he darted his tongue in and out of my honey. Damn, he had a gift.

The longer he licked and pulled on my clit, the longer I gave him head. His cock began to swell and I continued to suck. His cum spurted into my mouth as I slowly sucked him while I tightly gripped his cock. His arms wrapped around my hips, pulling my pussy deeper into his face. After he came, I tried to get up but he continued to lick my pussy. So, I continued to suck his limp cock. Within minutes, he was back up and ready to go. Jeremy pushed me up and bent me over the couch. My face went down and my ass up. He entered my kingdom and pounded away at me. He went deeper and deeper as I yelled out for more. After about fifteen minutes of serious pounding, he pulled out and came all over my ass and back. After he drained himself, he stuck his face back in my pussy and licked a few more times. This time, I busted right in his face. That's what he wanted me to do; my king was satisfied.

After we had sex, we showered together. Then Jeremy put on his clothes and left me looking stupid again. He didn't say goodbye bitch or nothing; just got his nut and left. Damn, I felt so fucking dumb, but it was okay because I loved him so much.

"Bitch, how many times are you going to say it's okay for him to treat you that way?" Nikki butted into my thoughts.

"He loves me," I argued.

"Bullshit. He loves the sex you are giving him; all the sucking and fucking. You downgrade yourself so fucking low. That's why I can't stand your weak ass," Nikki belittled me.

"Don't talk like that Nikki. You are the only one who really loves me. Please don't say stuff like that," I pleaded.

"Damn, I wish you'd stop all that damn whining. I will always love you and don't forget that," Nikki said.

"I won't Nikki. Just promise you will protect me," I said.

"Always," Nikki assured me.

After I had eaten supper, I grabbed my comforter and a pillow off the bed. I was sleeping on the couch tonight. I wanted to lay there where Jeremy had left his scent of Tommy Sport cologne. His scent would give me a good feeling all night long. As I lay down, I could smell his cum everywhere, and it was loud. He had a scent that drove me crazy; it drove me like a mad woman trying to get out of a mental institution.

I snuggled into my comforter while looking at the television, as I tried to fall asleep. The images of tonight with Jeremy re-played over and over in my head. Deep down, I knew that Jeremy loved me; he just didn't know how to love me. If he'd give me the chance, I would show him that it is very easy. We could have an unconditional love like *Bonnie and Clyde*. We both would ride and die for each other, and would protect each other from harm; just loving each other like no tomorrow. Damn, I wished he would give me that chance back again. It is okay; I wouldn't stop until he gave me what I was looking for. But tonight, I am happy for the moment.

"Nicole, are you happy?" Nikki asked.

"Yes, I'm so happy that Jeremy came over and spent time with me," I replied.

"Well, I feel better that you are not crying," Nikki said.

"I can't cry. Did you hear Jeremy say that he wanted to make sure I was safe?" I asked Nikki.

"Yes, I heard him. Just remember I'm the only one who can protect you. I love you too much," Nikki responded.

"Yes, I know Nikki. I know you love me and I love you too," I replied.

"Good," Nikki said.

Chapter 4

The next day, Leslie and I met at the office; Leslie was a good friend of mine. I met Leslie when I first came to Las Vegas to practice law, and we decided to become partners in a firm called the Webb & Lee Law Firm. She was already established before I came along, and she decided to bring me on. Leslie Lee graduated from Las Vegas State University in the top of her class. She'd had nothing but straight A's in high school and in college; she was just that smart. Leslie was thirty-one years old, so she had been a little hesitant about hiring me as a partner, since I was seven years younger than her; but it didn't matter to me. I did my job. I showed her all of my certificates, awards, and my Juris Doctorate degree from the University of Seattle. She stated that she would give me a chance to show her my skills. Even if I worked there or not, she still could stand on her own two feet, because she had millions of dollars. Bitch wasn't hurting for nothing. I figured she just felt sorry for me since I was new in town. Her job was more complicated than mine; I handled cases and lawsuits for The University of Las Vegas, while she took on criminal cases. So, a lot of times her job had her out of town working.

Leslie was on top of her game. She had three houses; one in Vegas, one in Los Angeles, and one in Miami. She had money and a lot of men. Even though she was rich, her friends still bought her gifts. Her motto was, "why fuck for free when you can get rich with Grade A pussy?" I always said she was selling pussy, but she

told me not to look at it that way. She said men want to fuck, and women are trying to get rich; it's an even trade.

"Girl, I heard about your accident. Sorry I couldn't get by to see you," she stated.

"Well, luckily I didn't die," I jokingly replied.

"You are crazy. I'm glad you didn't either. So, what's been going on?" she asked.

"Nothing; just the usual," I said.

"I know what that means," she said knowingly.

"What?" I asked.

"So, you and Jeremy are back on again?" she asked.

"Leslie, I don't know what to tell you. One minute he wants me, and the next, he's up in another bitch's face," I replied.

"Leave that broke ass mutha-fucker alone. I have a few good men you can meet," she stated.

"That's not a bad idea," I said thoughtfully.

"But?" she asked.

"But, I want to see what Jeremy is going to do; I think there is a good chance," I replied.

"Not shit; that's what he's going to do. You can do better than him Nicole," Leslie said.

"Maybe; maybe not," I replied.

"Well boo, let me know when you get tired of his monkey ass. I will hook you up with plenty of ballers who don't mind breaking you off," she boasted as she danced around the office.

"I will remember that," I said.

I grabbed my suitcase and walked out of the office. She was being a real bitch, and I didn't want to get ignorant. How was she going to tell me about my man? I wondered how she would feel when I decided to leave her company; I would let her know on down the road. I can't watch Jeremy, and do all this work shit for the hospital at the same time. Then she wants monthly paperwork; all this bullshit is too much for me. She will probably be pissed off with me because I'm leaving the company early, since I'm on a one year trial. She will get over it.

I got into my Mercedes and drove off. The hospital would see me tomorrow; today I needed to see what was going on with Jeremy. I might not be the only one, but I would damn sure try to be.

As I pulled up to Jeremy's house, I saw Lucy's car in his driveway. Instead of passing by, I pulled in. As I walked up to the door to ring the door bell, it opened.

"Oh shit, hey Nicole. You spooked me," said Jeremy.

"Why are you all jumpy and shit?" I asked.

"Shit nothing. I didn't hear you pull in the driveway," he replied.

"What's up? I dropped by to see if you were alright, since I haven't heard from you," I said.

"My bad, girl; just been a little busy. Well, come in," he invited.

I looked around to see if he had any KY Jelly lying around, or any other toys he played with. The baby oil was sitting out, so I guess I'd interrupted them. Sitting by the bar was Lucy. I gave her this "bitch get out of here" look, and she put her head down. I was pissed because she was invading my territory. This was my pasture, and I was the only bull that was going to rage around the mutha-fucker.

"Nicole, I want you to meet Lucy. Lucy this is Nicole," he introduced us. She got up to shake my hand, but I didn't extend my hand. I just turned back around to Jeremy. "Who is this?" I asked.

"Lucy is a friend of mine," he stated.

"You mean a fuck partner," I boldly said.

"Girl, what the fuck did you say? Stop fucking around, and come have a drink with us," he replied with this silly look on his face.

Lucy looked upset, but I didn't give a fuck. I wasn't going to hide the fact that I didn't want her there. He wanted me to pretend like we were friends. I could tell by the expression on his face, because he kept giving me this evil look.

"Nicole, Jeremy tells me that you are a lawyer," Lucy said.

"Why you ask? Do you need one?" I replied.

"I'm sorry, I didn't mean any harm," she apologized.

"Nicole, stop acting like such a bitch towards my guest, or I'm going to throw your ass out," Jeremy objected.

"Throw me out? You have lost your damn mind," I retorted.

"No, I'm so serious. Stop being rude to Lucy; you don't even know her," he replied.

"You are right. I'm so sorry Lucy. I'm just a little upset because you fucking my man," I blurted out.

Jeremy spit up vodka everywhere and Lucy almost choked.

"Your man? We are friends; remember Nicole?" Jeremy asked.

"Yeah, that's what you wanted, not me. I enjoy fucking you more than just as a friend," I said.

Jeremy jumped up, grabbed me by the arm and rushed me to the door. He was holding me very tight, so I could tell that he was very angry now. He shouldn't have had that bitch over anyway.

"So, you are throwing me out over a bitch?" I asked.

"She's my guest. If you don't know how to treat a guest in my house, then you will leave," he angrily replied.

"Go ahead and throw me out. You're not going to be satisfied until I fuck you up," I threatened.

"Bye Nicole; get your ass out of here," he rudely responded.

"Fuck you too, Jeremy," I replied softly while walking to my car. There he went with that nasty ass attitude, just like Marvin. Well, I guess I would have to show him who was boss around this bitch. I'd had all I could take from these rude ass men thinking they could run over me. I sat down in my car, and cranked it up. I began revving the engine over and over and over, until Jeremy came back outside. I let my window up as he came rushing towards the car.

"Nicole, stop fucking around, and get out of here. What the fuck has gotten into you?" he yelled.

"I'm so tired of you treating me like I ain't shit when it comes to other women," I replied.

"Bitch, we are just friends who fuck on a regular basis. If you can't handle this dick, then I will have to let you go. Now, stop acting like a bitch and go home," he stated.

I opened the car door and jumped out, "You stop acting like a bitch. I'm so tired of you using me," I said.

"Using you? You want it too, so don't act like it's all on me. I invited your ass in to sit down with us and you started talking stupid. I don't appreciate that shit," he stated.

"Well, you might fuck her tonight, but she doesn't have good pussy like I do. She will never fuck you like I do," I said.

"I don't know, but I'll find out tonight. Now, get the fuck out of here before I call the police," Jeremy threatened as he walked away from the car.

"Call the police. I don't give a fuck," I yelled out.

I got in my car and drove off. My tires were spinning all over the pavement. He had really pissed me off. I stopped by Pizza Hut before I proceeded home and grabbed take-out. I kept calling Jeremy's phone, but that bitch wouldn't pick up. Call me crazy; that nigga belonged to me. I called him about twenty-eight times before I decided to stop calling.

I had arrived at home, put on some jogging pants with a white Ike beater, and had begun eating on my Italian sausage pizza when the hospital called.

"Good evening, Ms. Webb. How are you doing?" Dr. John Lange spoke through the phone.

"Hello. I'm wonderful sir. What can I do for you?" I asked.

"Ms. Webb, we need your signature on two pieces of paperwork before we send if off," Dr. John Lange replied.

"I've finished all of the paperwork. What type of paper do you want me to sign?" I asked him.

"It's a waiver form that the hospital has created this month," he responded.

"Yes sir. Do you need the signatures this evening?" I asked.

"Yes ma'am, I do need them today, because we want to go ahead and proceed with this case," he answered.

"Okay. I'm about to get dressed and will be there in about half an hour," I told him.

Before leaving, I decided to play with my pussy before I left. I could imagine Jeremy banging this pussy. I had the movie *Stuffing Every Hole* playing on the big screen as I took out my leopard print dildo and inserted it into my pussy. I pinned my legs back while fucking myself. The harder the guy on the screen banged, the harder I pushed within myself. For a few minutes, I got mine. Then I washed off and proceeded to the hospital to sign the paperwork Dr. Lange wanted me to.

Upon arriving at the hospital, Dr. Lange also wanted me to look over a few things regarding this lawsuit we had with a lady in Iuka, Mississippi who was suing the hospital because she said they were responsible for killing her son. Her son had a heart transplant, and it worked for about two days. Suddenly, it quit for no reason, and now she wanted fifty millions dollars from the hospital.

Chapter 5

After leaving the hospital, my mind told me to go by Jeremy's house again. That bitch was probably still there. As I drove past, I noticed the lights were off, and her car was still parked in the driveway. I began beating my steering wheel while driving.

"Calm down bitch. You don't want to end up back in the hospital again," Nikki spoke.

"Fuck it. Nikki, she's there. She's there," I said.

"Let's break into his house and off both of them," Nikki suggested.

"What if I get caught?" I asked.

"You won't get caught; I have your back. Now be a woman, and do what you got to do," Nikki said.

"I can't do it Nikki," I admitted.

"I said that I would always protect you. Now, get out the fucking car," Nikki pressed.

"Suppose Jeremy is awake," I stalled.

"Then you take him out too," Nikki said.

"No, I don't want to hurt Jeremy. My love is too strong," I protested.

"I'm so tired of hearing you talk about love. Bitch, this woman is in there fucking your man, and you out in the car talking about you love him. Go do it or I will," Nikki demanded.

My mind was running in all different kinds of directions. All I could hear was Nikki's voice saying, "kill that bitch." I parked about half a mile up the street and walked back down to Jeremy's house. I crept up by the balcony doors; he always kept them unlocked. It didn't matter if he did or didn't though, because I had made a key a long time ago. He couldn't keep me out even if he wanted to.

I slowly opened the balcony doors and stepped in. My heart began to pound a little harder as I tried to listen for anything.

"Stop bitch; you have to be calm," Nikki said.

"Not now Nikki," I said.

"We need this kill bitch. We've been waiting too long for this," she kept saying.

"I'm not hurting Jeremy," I said.

"Stop saying that, I'm not hurting Jeremy, bullshit. Didn't that nigga throw you out of his house today because of this bitch?" she asked.

"You are right; but that's no reason to hurt him," I said.

"Bitch, we're going to do this my way," Nikki replied.

"Okay, but I'm not hurting Jeremy," I repeated.

I continued down the hall to his bedroom. The bedroom door was wide open; in his big king sized bed, he and Lucy lay naked on top of the covers. The rage came rushing in, and I knew there was no more turning back now. I turned around, walked away from the room, and headed to the kitchen to get a knife. I leaned against the counter trying to catch my breath.

"Bitch, don't you pass out on me now. What the fuck is wrong with you?" Nikki asked.

"I can't seem to calm down," I told Nikki as I looked down at my hands, which were badly shaking.

"You just nervous; I said that I will protect you. Now, take your ass back down the hall," Nikki told me.

I knew he had a huge kitchen knife, so I eased the drawer open, took the knife out and headed back to the bedroom. I was walking slowly because I was still trying to catch my breath.

Stepping back up to the door, I saw Lucy lying on her back, with her legs slightly open while Jeremy was lying on his stomach. As I walked up to the bed, I lifted the knife in the air to stab that whore, but couldn't. Nikki wanted me to stab her in the neck, and pin her to the bed. If I did, then Jeremy would wake up. I took the knife and put it to her pussy. Maybe I should stab her there, so she couldn't ever fuck again; not my man anyway. The tip of the knife grazed her pussy, and she turned over towards Jeremy. I ducked down quickly. My heart began to race again; I had to get

out. My heart was thumping so hard, I could hear every beat. I had to get the fuck out. Fuck what Nikki wanted me to do. I ran out of the room and down the hall to the kitchen. I was leaning against his kitchen sink about ready to throw up.

"Don't you give us away! Get a hold of yourself. You acting like a dumb ass," Nikki mocked.

"I can't do this. I can't kill that girl," I said.

"Yes you can, and you will," Nikki said.

"You do it Nikki. I can't," I refused.

"Bitch, you have the knife in your hand. What's so different from the other kill we did together?" she asked.

"I guess there is no difference," I admitted.

"Hell no. Just kill the bitch and get it over with," Nikki stated.

Before I could start back toward the bedroom, I heard something coming from down the hall. I had to hide back behind a wall in the kitchen, and my heart started beating fast again. It seemed like it was beating so hard, that I could feel it in my throat.

"Damn, somebody is up," I said to myself. At that time, I didn't hear Nikki say a word. What happened? My heart was pumping and I was about to piss on myself. If Jeremy caught me, he would beat the shit out of me. I leaned very close to the wall, hoping whoever it was didn't see me.

The person was tiptoeing down the hallway. My eyes opened wider to see, and I saw it was Lucy. She had her clothes and purse

in her hand, about to leave without saying goodbye. She stood in the living room to dress, and I slowly tiptoed behind her. This time it was all me; Nikki was nowhere around. She was right; I would get the feel of it on my own. It was scary, but it felt good. Lucy was still naked when I put the knife to her throat.

"Bitch, don't say a word, or I will kill you right here," I hissed.

"Please don't," she whimpered.

"Shut the fuck up," I spoke roughly as I pushed the knife to her neck. She let out a low cry.

"Move bitch," I continued.

We moved slowly towards the door. I saw a hammer on the table. I slowly picked it up and put it in my back like a gun, while still holding the knife to her neck. I closed the door behind us slowly, and we moved toward her car.

"I'm so sorry if I've done anything to you," she said.

"Stop whining, you fucking pussy. Did you enjoy fucking my man tonight?" I asked.

"Nicole, is that you?" she asked while sobbing.

"Who did you think it was bitch?" I asked nastily.

I leaned her against her car with the knife to the back of her neck, ready to go in deep.

"Spread your legs bitch," I demanded.

"What?" she asked.

She got on her knees, and I took the hammer out of my back. She turned to her side and I lost it. *Bang, bang, bang.* Right up side her mutha-fucking head. I hit that bitch so hard, all she did was let out a low sigh as she fell to the ground on her stomach. She smelled like piss. I looked around to see if anyone was watching; it didn't hit me until then to look around. Damn.

She began to moan. I thought I'd killed her, because with that second and third blow, I'd heard her skull crack. As she lay on the ground naked, I just looked at her. I looked at my knife, and kneeled down on the ground between her legs. As I moved her legs farther apart, I began to fondle her pussy. Then I rubbed both ass cheeks, trying to get the feel of what Jeremy did. I had the knife in my right hand; I spread her ass cheeks with my left hand, and then put the knife to her ass.

"Go ahead and do it," Nikki cheered on.

"Now, you're here," I said.

"Bitch, I was with you the whole time. I just wanted you to get the feel of the kills we do. This bitch had your man and you finally reacted. Damn, it took a very long time for you to see what I was talking about," Nikki continued.

Before Nikki could finish talking; I shoved that knife right up Lucy's ass. Her head jerked up and fell back down slowly. I sliced down to her pussy, and blood spurted out on me. I looked up the street to see if anyone was coming. I looked back down at Lucy, stabbed her right at the top of her ass bone, and then sliced downward to her open ass. Blood was really spurting out now. I

wanted to cut that bitch to pieces right there, but couldn't. I had spent too much time there out in the open.

I opened her car door and struggled to put her inside. Luckily, she wasn't a big girl; just had a big juicy ass. Sweat was pouring off me like I'd run a ten mile marathon. There was sweat and blood running all over me, and my clothes were soaked.

I ran over to the passenger side and pulled her over, trying to straighten her up. Her monkey ass was losing blood everywhere. I had to lay the seat all the way back to get her over there. Once I got her straight, I got in on the driver's side and drove away. I drove to Vegas Heights, a cliff where people go to fuck. As I drove near the edge of the cliff, it seemed like she was moving around or something. Her eyes pierced me, as I hit the gas and jumped out of the car. I hit the ground rolling like a bowling ball. That BMW went flying off the cliff like in the movies. All I could hear was that bitch screaming, and it sounded like music to my ears. That should teach her a lesson about fucking with other women's men. I ran over to the cliff and looked down as the car exploded. Balls and balls of fire blazed from the car, and black smoke filled the air. The car was popping and melting down to pieces. I looked down at my clothes; they were covered with blood and dirt. How in the hell was I going to hide this shit? As I stood there, a memory came to mind.

"Baby girl, you look so pretty in your new dress," my father said, as he grabbed my arms and swung me around in circles.

"Thank you daddy for buying my new dress," I replied.

"You deserve the best," he said.

"Why you didn't get anything to wear for church?" I asked.

"Well, your mother didn't think I needed anything. Plus, I have enough clothes in my closet," he answered.

"You are the best father in the world," I said.

"Thank you, baby girl. You are the best daughter in the world," he replied.

We danced in circles until I was tired. That day my mama bought Vanessa two dresses for church, and didn't buy me anything. She said I had too many, but Vanessa had just as many. After my father and I danced, we sat at the kitchen table eating cookies 'n cream ice cream. He fixed two big bowls. We sat and were eating before my mama came in screaming at him that I didn't deserve any ice cream. She grabbed my bowl and poured the ice cream into the kitchen sink. Her tongue was very sharp; she didn't care if she hurt your feelings or not. I ran out of the kitchen, and into the big brown barn crying. I climbed the small wooden stairs, lay on the hay, and cried and cried. She hated the fact that my father loved me more than her.

My father came into the barn after me and said, "Now you know your mama didn't mean what she said."

"She's always mean to me when you're not around," I cried. "I hate her."

"Don't say that about your mama! She loves you; just has a strange way of showing it," my father said.

Suddenly, my mind snapped back to the present. Looking at the explosion had caused me to have a flashback about home. After watching the car burn; I began to walk back to my car. I began to pick up the pace when I saw headlights coming from behind me. Luckily, they were far off. I dove into the bushes and rolled down this small hill. After coming to a stop down the hill, I began to crawl back up to look for the car. I figured it would stop because of the burning car, but it kept flying right past. As soon as I topped the hill, the car rushed past me. I lay down on the ground and waited for the car lights to disappear, then I jumped up running. It seemed like I was getting lightheaded; then my mind went blank.

Chapter 6

I woke up rubbing my head wondering what had happened to me. My feet touched the floor, then I jumped straight up in the air as I remembered last night. I checked out my clothes, but there was no blood anywhere; I was dressed in my night clothes. I ran to the bathroom, but saw no evidence of blood. I ran to the kitchen and also found nothing. What the hell was really going on? I ran to my other bedroom, only to find nothing. I was racking my brain trying to remember what the hell had happened. The only thing I could remember was watching Lucy's car drive off the cliff as her screams rang out into the air; from there, I'm clueless.

There was a loud knock at the door, and it almost scared me shitless. I walked slowly over to the door as someone banged harder.

"Nicole, open this fucking door!" Jeremy screamed.

I ran over to the door and swung it open. "What?" I asked.

"Girl, I think I'm in some shit. I can't remember a damn thing that happened last night. Lucy and I popped a few roofies, and now she's gone," he replied.

"What do you mean she's gone?" I asked Jeremy.

"Nicole, the bitch is missing," he said.

"How do you know that?" I asked.

"Because her sister called me early this morning. I told her that she must have left in the middle of the night, because when I woke up she was gone," he said while pacing my floor.

"She probably went elsewhere," I said.

"Girl, this ain't the time to play around. After I woke up, I saw my hammer, a knife and some blood and shit in a bucket sitting at my patio door," he continued.

"It is all your stuff," I pointed out.

"Hell yeah. All of that shit is mine, but I couldn't hurt anybody," he said.

"Where is all that stuff now?" I asked.

"It's in my car," he replied.

"Damn, are you stupid? That's the first place the police would look!" I exclaimed.

"The police? I didn't hurt her," he said.

"Damn, I will help you this time," I said.

I got his keys and walked down to the car; I was the happiest woman in the world. My man had come to me for help. He could have gone anywhere else, but he came to me. That let me know that I was becoming an important person in his life; he needed me to protect him. I felt damn good.

"Bitch, what the fuck are you doing? This nigga don't want you. He's only here so you can take the rap," Nikki said.

"Well, you should have planned better. This is your entire fault," I said.

"My fault? Bitch, I did what I thought was best. Now you want to save a whore. Fuck that pussy ass mutha-fucker. We are in this together, and I feel like you're turning your back on me," Nikki replied.

"How? You have always been there for me," I said.

I looked up toward the balcony and saw Jeremy staring down at me.

"Who the fuck you talking to?" he asked.

"Nobody," I said.

"You're a fucking lie. You are talking to somebody," he pressed.

"Go back inside and stop bullshitting," I said.

"Bitch, stop fucking around. You better not be trying to set me up," he responded.

"Nigga, please," I said.

I gathered all the stuff, and brought the bucket back up to my apartment with all the things in it. Jeremy was sitting on the couch looking like a lost puppy.

"You trying to set me up," he accused as he jumped up off the couch.

"You're just paranoid. Why would I set you up?" I asked while carrying the bucket.

"What the fuck? Why would you bring it up here?" he asked jumpily.

"How else am I going to get rid of it? Just go home. I will handle everything," I assured him.

"How can I trust you to get rid of this shit? You might turn me in," he said.

"Are you fucking serious? You came to me with all this bullshit. Apparently, you trust me because you wouldn't be here telling me this shit otherwise," I said.

He didn't ask any questions, just bolted out of my door. Jeremy was so fucking weak. I tried to think how in the hell did I do all this, then I realized it was that damn Nikki. Since I wouldn't kill Jeremy, she was trying to frame him for all this.

"Stop fucking with me Nikki; this shit ain't funny. Leave Jeremy alone!" I yelled out to her. I knew she could hear me.

"Bitch, you are so dumb. He brought the evidence to you so you can go down with him," Nikki said.

"Jeremy loves me. That's why he came to me; he trusts me," I responded.

"Stupid, stupid, stupid," Nikki said apathetically. "I put this shit on him, and you're trying to protect him. Well bitch, I'm trying to

protect you, but you're making this shit very hard to do," Nikki continued.

"Nikki, don't get mad at me," I begged.

"I'm already furious with you. Stop trying to help this pussy ass nigga; he doesn't want you. He's making you look like a damn fool," Nikki ranted.

"Please Nikki, don't say that. You are just jealous because he doesn't want you," I said.

"Bitch, I will kill him, and then you won't have him. You keep pushing my buttons, and I will do just that. Kill him," Nikki threatened.

After I got dressed, I put the bucket into my car and just drove. Finally, I made it to the Midnight Vegas Bridge. I stopped my car on the side for emergency vehicles. People passing in cars were looking at me like I was crazy, so I turned on my hazard lights. I walked to the passenger side of the vehicle, and pulled out the evidence. I threw it over the bridge, and watched as the contents hit the river. The bucket filled with water and began to sink. Just as it was doing that, a police car pulled up behind me. I began to panic and sat on the edge turning my legs out towards the water. The police officer ran up to me.

"Ma'am, do you know it's very dangerous for you to hang out here?" he asked.

"Sir, I'm just hanging out looking at the view," I lied to him.

"This is not the way to go. Just come down, and I will see about getting some help for you," he said.

"I don't need any help. I am just sightseeing," I replied.

"Ma'am, please come down," he urged.

"Are you going to lock me up? I did nothing wrong; just looking over the ledge at the water," I said.

"Nobody is going to lock you up. Just come down off the ledge. You have plenty of things to do besides looking over a ledge. Do you know it looks like you're trying to commit suicide?" he asked.

"Things like what? There is nothing wrong with this view; I like it up here. The wind is blowing, and the air smells good," I hedged.

"Ma'am, I understand that, but you need to get your ass down off that ledge now. I won't ask you again," he said.

I began to try to think about happy times, but couldn't think of any, except for the memories of my father. "Well Officer, I don't want to piss you off today, so I'm coming down off the ledge. Don't shoot me," I responded.

"Get your ass down off the ledge Lady. I'm not going to keep asking you," he repeated.

I stood up on the ledge, and for the first time thought about actually killing myself. This big gray bridge couldn't hold me. Then thoughts began to run through my mind; is my life worth living?

"Ma'am, please. I'm begging you to come down. I apologize for cursing you. I need you to come down," the officer pleaded.

"Don't move another step, or I will jump. Move back toward your patrol car and I will get down," I told him. Before I could get down, I looked out into traffic, and saw this little red haired girl staring at me as their vehicle slowly drove by. She put her hand up on the window as if to say hello or goodbye. This brought back a memory of when my mother took Vanessa to the fair that was in town. My father said I could go, but my mother lied and said I had poor grades at school, so she said I had to stay home. That was my punishment. My mother and Vanessa climbed into the car and were ready to go. My father stood in the passenger doorway and looked up at me. I put my hand on the window wanting him to stay, but then I heard my mother screaming at him to get in. My father blew me a kiss and got in the car. I placed both my hands on the window and cried that day. I cried and cried until they came back home hours later.

"Ma'am," a voice called out.

I snapped back to reality, and realized the officer was standing next to his car waiting on me to get down.

"I'm sorry sir, I'm getting down," I spoke as I dropped myself off the ledge and onto the street.

"Thank God," the officer spoke out loud.

I looked at the police officer; he looked scared out of his mind. So, I decided to stop playing games, since the bucket had disappeared into the water. I looked down the street toward the

van that had driven past with the little girl looking out at me. My mind wondered if she was being mistreated too.

"You really scared me," the officer said as he approached me.

"I'm so sorry officer; I guess I wasn't thinking." I replied.

"Do you want me to get you some help? Let me take you down to the precinct," he offered.

"No sir, I'm really okay; I was just sightseeing, not trying to commit suicide," I said.

"Are you sure? Because our department has people to help you," he said.

"I'm sure," I said as I gave the officer a hug.

"Sir, I'm so sorry for getting up on the ledge. I know it's strange that I would get on the ledge of a bridge, but I just wasn't thinking. I'm sorry for scaring you. To be honest, I scared myself," I stated as I cracked a smile.

He smiled back at me. I pulled away from him and headed to my car. As I entered my car, I saw another patrol car pulling up. The officer jumped out waving for me to stop. I looked in his face and knew this was going to be a long process. *Damn, damn, damn.* I rolled the window down and he walked up asking, "Ma'am, were you the lady on the ledge of this bridge?"

"Yes sir it was me, but I was just sightseeing; that's it. Why is everyone making a big issue of me sightseeing?" I spoke in a near hostile tone.

"We got a call saying a lady was on the bridge trying to commit suicide," he explained.

"No sir. I explained it to that officer over there. I wasn't trying to hurt myself. I love myself too much to take my life. I'm so sorry that you all got this call, but I'm good," I tried to explain. The officer looked at me as if he didn't believe shit I was saying. He looked back at the other officer. The officer gave him a nod and he walked away. I figured he would pull me out of the car and take me to jail; or maybe get me out the car and have a long talk with me, but he didn't do anything after the other officer nodded his head. I guess that was some kind of signal. I waved goodbye to him, and I drove off. Shit, that was very close. Fucking around with Jeremy, and I almost got busted for his stupid ass. There was no way I was letting him go now. This would bond us together for life. Every time he wanted to leave; I would remind him of what I did for him. He's weak; he'll fall for anything.

I drove down the highway like a bat out of hell, and I noticed that traffic was moving very slowly. I turned on the radio and Nelly's song *Gone,* featuring Kelly Rowland, was blasting out of the speakers. My heart began to melt as I thought about Jeremy. This little incident would really put me in the game with him. As the song played, I remembered the good times we'd had. There was one incident that stood out more than anything. I was driving his Dodge Magnum down the highway as that song blasted, and he began to sing the song to me. He was dancing around in his seat in a happy mood; at that time we were dating.

He began to touch all over my body as I drove his car. Jeremy looked as if he was so in love with me. There was that connection

between us that nobody could break; I was his and he was mine. I didn't care if he fucked thousands of bitches; I would always be his number one woman. That day he made me feel so lucky, and so happy to be with him. I think I fell deeper in love with him. He was looking so handsome in his Sean John pants, shirt, and shoes. Every time he put on an outfit, you better believe he was dressed to kill. That's why so many women wanted him. Then he smelled so good all the time too. Even when he was hanging out around the house, he was dressed and smelling good.

"That song was for you, Shawty," Jeremy said as he finished singing to me that day.

"Oh really?" I asked.

"Hell yeah. You will always be my girl," he replied.
"Are you sure about that?" I asked.

"Yes I'm sure. You will always be my number one," he said.

"Good. I will hold you to that," I said very seriously.

Chapter 7

From that day forward, I thought Jeremy would be a changed man, but he was still a fucking dog. He was still fucking bitches and treating me like I was shit. My love for Jeremy became so deep that I quit my job. Leslie was so pissed off with me, she probably thought about kicking my ass, but she knew I wasn't going down easy.

"Nicole, do you realize it took me weeks to decide to bring you on as a partner?" Leslie disappointedly asked.

"I know, Leslie. I decided to move back to my hometown because my mother is very ill and needs me," I lied.

"I understand you have to take care of your mom; why are you just now telling me she's sick?" Leslie questioned.

"I didn't want everyone to know she was sick. Plus, I figured my sister Vanessa would take care of her, but she can't do it by herself," I spoke the perfect lie.

"Well, I'm disappointed that you are leaving. I wish you would have given me enough notice to hire somebody else, but it's all good. With or without someone, this firm is still going to stand," she said.

"Yes, I know Leslie," I replied.

Leslie walked back into her office and closed the door. I knew that bitch was pissed off at me, but I didn't give a fuck. I understand she gave me a chance to be a partner, but it's not like she was going to be hurting. That bitch was succeeding alone, before I even came along. She would be alright when the swelling went down.

After I quit, it felt so good. I had plenty of money, so I wasn't hurting for anything. My only thoughts were of loving Jeremy and being there whenever he needed me. That boy just didn't know how deep my love was. It became so intense, that I was willing to die for that nigga. I wanted him to be all mine and nothing was going to stop me. Now, he was about to make me fucking snap. How many more bitches did he want to die? If he kept fucking with Nikki, he'd be in a body bag. I couldn't always control this crazy bitch; she was beginning to become more than I could handle.

I was at the crib chilling when Jeremy's tracking device started going off. He was on the move, and it looked like he was headed toward this bitch Dena's house. For the last couple of weeks, it had been Dena this and Dena that. Fuck Dena. I'm the one he should be talking about.

Jeremy talked to me almost every day about different women. When was he going to wake up and realize that he had a good woman in front of him? I did any and everything he asked me, and he knew my love ran deep. I tried to think of why he rejected me. Was I that bad of a person that he couldn't love me like I needed? Was I not worthy of his love? He had a woman who loved him, a woman who was willing to kill for him, and a woman who was willing to die for him.

It makes me fucking sick to look at pussy ass niggas that want bitches that don't give a fuck about them. Someone who treats them any kind of way; a bitch who loves fucking the whole neighborhood. A gold digging bitch, who's all about her mutha-fucking self; a bitch who is more worried about her financial stability than the nigga she is treating badly. Jeremy deserved to be treated better than that. That whore he was fucking was all about that paper. He was so unwilling to see what was really going on. I loved him more than myself and would give him the world. What's so bad about that? Fuck it. That's his stupid ass getting played.

I jumped in my car with my device, and headed out to follow Jeremy. I'd gotten so tired of this shit with Dena. She didn't want Jeremy; only his money. It's true he didn't work, but everyone knew he was paid. His father died years ago and left him millions. Every woman he fucked was after money. I guess it felt good to him to help gold digging ass females, but if it wasn't for his finances, his relationships would all crumble. He would pay those whores hundreds just for some pussy, when he could easily fuck me for free. I guess it isn't as good when it's free.

I was driving down Highway 784 when the device stopped beeping. I was looking and driving, all at the same time; about to kill myself. After a few minutes of looking, I realized that he was at Dena's house. I threw the tracking device on the seat and hit the gas. My mutha-fucking blood was boiling. Damn, I should run up in this bitch's house and start busting.

"Bitch, I told you he should die," Nikki spoke.

"No. Not Jeremy," I said.

"No. Not Jeremy," Nikki sarcastically mocked me.

"Bitch, let me run this shit. Leave me the fuck alone, before I kill you," I retorted.

"That's my girl. You are starting to love the feeling. I've been trying to get you to wake up for years. Blood gives me the taste to kill, and now you taste it," Nikki said gleefully.

"You want me to taste it, but I don't. I can't harm innocent people like you," I denied.

"Just wait. You have the taste for it, because you want to hurt Dena," Nikki said.

I looked in the rearview mirror and saw Nikki sitting in the back seat. She had this evil smile on her face. As I turned back to driving, my mind started going haywire. All I could hear was Jeremy's voice in my head talking about being friends, while he fucked other women. It kept going on and on in my head; how he kept saying he didn't love me. After all this shit I was going through just for us to be together, there was no fucking way I would be without him.

Finally, I rode past Dena's house and saw his baby blue Dodge Magnum parked in the driveway. He had never backed it in before. As I drove past, Nikki began to get very angry. This nigga had pushed me too far. I would not stand by and watch him make a fool out of me. I'd had all I could take.

My mind was racing. I decided to go across town to purchase a few gallons of gas, because I was going to burn her house down

with both of them in there. I didn't give a fuck anymore. If I couldn't have him; nobody could.

I drove for miles and miles outside of town; it would be too risky to purchase gas inside of town. I pulled in at Lecky's Convenience Store, and purchased a gallon of gas.

"Hi there Miss Lady," a short old gray haired man greeted me.

"Hello sir," I replied.

"How are you doing on this summer night?" he asked.

"I'm doing great sir, how are you?" I asked.

"I'm here," he replied.

"Great. I need a gallon of gas, so I can mow my yard," I lied.

"Mow your yard? Where is your husband?" he asked.

"I don't have one sir. I don't have a boyfriend either, so I have to do it all by myself," I responded.

"Oh okay. Well, I'm available if you will have me," he joked.

"Really? How old are you?" I asked.

"What does age have to do with it?" he shot back.

"It has a lot to do with it. You are my daddy's age; what can I do with you?" I sarcastically asked.

I smiled at him and proceeded out the door to get my gas. The old man gave me a gallon jug, and I filled that bitch to the top. Then I continued on to three more gas stations, and got three

more gallons of gas. Jeremy would see if I was a stupid bitch. He wouldn't hurt me and think he could get away. I'm the type of woman who loves to seek revenge. It pisses me off for a man to use a woman. Now that I have Nikki on my side to protect me, I'm untouchable.

After getting all that gas, I drove back to Dena's house; Jeremy's car was gone. I turned on my tracking device, and it showed he was at The Olive Garden downtown. He must have taken her out to dinner, or he might have gone by himself. He loves The Olive Garden; that is his favorite restaurant. I bet she didn't know that shit.

Dena didn't know how I looked, so I walked up to the door. I took the end of my shirt and pushed the doorbell. I couldn't take any chances with my fingerprints. Even though my plan was to burn this bitch down, I still had to be careful. I had been sloppy with Lucy and Marvin's deaths. This time I would be a little more careful.

Nobody was home, so I stepped all around the house, trying to find a way in. She had balcony doors on the back. I tried to open the doors, but they were locked. I looked around to see if anyone was watching. Nobody was out, so I kicked in the glass door. It took me three tries to break it. As the glass shattered to the ground, I stepped back, and looked around to make sure the neighbors didn't come out.

I stepped through the broken glass, and walked on it as I looked around. She was very messy. Clothes were everywhere, and the kitchen looked like a hog pen. The bitch was nasty. My heart began skipping beats like I was scared. About this time, I

was running from room to room looking. She wasn't there. Her bed was messed up, and I walked over and saw the covers were wet. I pulled the cover off the bed and sniffed it; I could smell Jeremy's cum. I guess he got himself a nut before he took that bitch out to eat. Something clicked in my head and it was on; I let Nikki do the damn thang. Nikki ran back and forward, carrying gallons of gas to burn that bitch down.

Nikki and I walked from room to room pouring gas on everything. She didn't want to miss anything. Dena's bed was the last thing I wanted to pour gas on. My mind went blank, as I just stood there staring. I could actually see him fucking her like he had with Lucy. He fucked the same old way every time. He loved getting his dick sucked, and busting a nut in their mouth. Damn, I wish it were me. As I poured gas on the bed, I cried.

"Bitch, are you getting weak on me?" Nikki asked.

"No Nikki," I sniffled.

"You have got to stop this crybaby shit. I'm getting sick of hearing you cry," Nikki said.

"Don't be like that!" I said.

"What you going to do? Cry, or burn this bitch down?" Nikki asked.

"I'm burning this bitch down," I said.

After I soaked everything, I ran to the balcony door. I made a small trail of gas leading out to the grass. I hesitated, but Nikki made sure I went through with it.

"Burn this mutha-fucker down. Now!" she urged.

I lit my match and tossed it on the ground. The fire started up slowly, and before it got to the house, I started running away from the house and toward my car; I didn't care who saw me. As soon as I got in the car, her whole house blazed up in flames. Black smoke was coming out of the roof and windows. I wanted to stay and watch, but Nikki didn't.

"Get out of here before we get caught!" Nikki screamed.

"No, you wanted this. Now watch," I said.

"Bitch, I'm not afraid of death, or dying. You are the weak one," Nikki said.

"I'm not weak Nikki. I just don't like hurting people," I corrected her.

"If that is true, then what are you doing now? You are burning this female's house down," Nikki pointed out.

I looked in the mirror and there was that evil smile on Nikki's face again. For the first time, I was feeling her. I'd been fighting Nikki since I was a child. She was in and out of my life as a child but not this strongly since Vanessa's three guy friends raped me. Vanessa brought them home one day to snort powder. That is a day I will never forget; I was twelve years old. They came into my room and fucked me. One boy held my left arm as another boy held down my right arm. This boy named James forced my panties off and took me first. After that, they took turns raping me. I tried to scream, but they held my mouth shut.

Vanessa was so stoned, she forgot about me, and that's why I blamed her. She'd said that she would always protect me, but she didn't. I hated her for letting her friends take my virginity. However, the thing that hurt me the most was the fact that Mama blamed me. She said I wanted them boys to fuck me, and that I had let them. I tried to tell her what happened, but she just beat me and locked me in my room. To make matters worse, even though I didn't realize it at first, my own parents were molesting me. I thought it was natural for a mother to caress her daughter in her special spot. She would come into my room sometimes and stick her finger down below; she would insert a finger inside of me, and it hurt. Each time she did this, she would lock me away in my room. When my father did this, he hurt me worse, but apologized for his actions. Mama would always make me get on my knees and pray to God. She would make me say that I was wrong for letting those boys fuck my pussy.

How can a mother be so cruel to her daughter? I was her baby, her child. She and Vanessa were to blame; they both were supposed to protect me. I wished my father was still living, because he wouldn't have let that happen to me. Those two walked around like nothing had happened to me. They treated me like dirt—like shit.

Nikki came into my life then, and has never left my side. She's the reason why I didn't go insane. So, why was I fighting with her so much? I wondered. I should embrace her in my life forever. Sometimes she would comfort me when my father came into my room at night. He would sing to me, as he touched my special spot like Mama did. Father hurt me, but unlike Mother, he would always apologize for what he had done.

For the first time, Nikki and I made eye contact. There was that deep connection she was looking for. I looked in the rear view mirror at Nikki and smiled back. Nicole was gone; a lost soul.

"Bitch, it's ON....................."

Chapter 8

After I handled business in Vegas, I drove home to Seattle, Washington. It was time I faced James, Kevin, and Keith. All this anger and hurt was because of them. There was no way I could go on with my life while they lived in peace. I wanted to make their life miserable, just like mine.

After driving for hours and hours, I finally arrived at my destination. My mind was so wired up, I couldn't sleep. Probably because I was geeked up from a couple of uppers I had taken. Fuck it.

I arrived at this old farmhouse that Marvin's mom owned in the country. I checked out the whole place; no one was there. It was the middle of the night, and I was awake digging up guns Marvin had buried. Nobody knew about them but him and me.

I dug and dug, but found nothing. I sat down on the ground, trying to make sure this was the right spot. Damn, I'd forgotten he'd moved them. I walked over to the barn; there was a trap door inside and underground where he'd hidden the guns. I pulled on the barn doors, and they were locked. I walked around to the other side, but those doors were locked as well. There was a small door on the side of the barn. I took a chance and pulled on it, and the door opened; I looked in and then proceeded to walk on in. I

walked around the barn trying to remember where the trap door was located. Finally, I found it. To my surprise there were many fucking guns. He had an Air Force Talon, Air Force Talon SS, an AK-47, a .50 Caliber, an M-16, and my specialty; the Air Soft Sniper Rifle. Other guns were also available; like the Glock 40, Glock 45, and a 9 mm pistol.

I didn't want to be greedy, so I gathered up the Air Soft Sniper Rifle, the Air Force Talon SS, and the 9 mm. It was amazing that nobody had found those guns after three years. I gathered my ammo and hid everything in the trunk of my car, by wrapping blankets around them; they were snuggled away safely.

I closed the trunk of the car, and began staring at the old house. A memory of Vanessa and me running around playing in our yard flashed before my eyes. She was the police, and I was the robber. She was chasing after me, trying to take me to jail and her mouth was wailing off like a real police siren. Suddenly, father walked outside and said, "Y'all gals sit down and stop all that yelling; your mama's trying to sleep." We both ran and jumped up on the edge of the porch. Father grabbed Vanessa by the hand, and they walked towards the barn.

"I want to go too," I told Father.

"No Nicole. It's Vanessa's turn to brush the horses today. Not yours. You will brush the horses tomorrow," he replied. Vanessa walked slowly behind Father. She looked back at me like she was very scared. I knew what he meant when he said he was going to brush the horses. Father would take me to the barn and fondle me. Sometimes he would get on top of me, and it hurt really, really bad. He told me to never tell anyone; it was our secret.

Father and Vanessa stayed in the barn a long time. I looked up into the window of the house and saw Mama just staring out toward the barn. She looked down at me with this evil look, snapped her head backward, and walked away. I moved to the steps on the porch, waiting for them to come out. It was getting dark and I could see the lamp light come on in the barn. All you could see was two shadows. I sat there as I saw Father on top of Vanessa, humping.

After a long time, he came out, but Vanessa was not with him. I jumped up and ran over to him. He grabbed my hand and turned me around to head back into the house.

"Where's Vanessa?" I asked.

"She has sinned, my child. She will have to stay out in the barn tonight. You just go inside the house and get ready for supper," he replied.

That night I sat in my room on the bed, and stared out the window at the barn. I knew Vanessa was scared, because I was scared when I stayed out there. My head began to hurt and these clicking noises kept sounding off. At the sound of the noises in my head, I snapped back to reality. I shook my head and proceeded towards the house.

I walked up and tried the door, but it was locked. I checked every door on the house, and they were all locked. There was a window in the back of the house, so I took a shovel from the small shed in back of the house and bust out the window. After removing all the glass from the window, I squeezed through it, and made my way into the old house. I took a bath and changed

into some old clothes. This house had been around for years; I believe it was probably about fifty years old. It was yellow and had green shutters; an odd color if you ask me. It looked like someone was keeping up the maintenance around here; the electricity and the water were still working. It was stupid, because nobody had lived here for years. I looked in the refrigerator, but found no food. Checked the cabinets, still no food. I wanted to drive into town and get me something to eat, but I couldn't because my body felt tired. I decided to lay down for a little while, and head out in the morning before day.

All during the night, I kept hearing all types of noises. Crickets were chirping, and it seemed like the house was popping. It had me paranoid like a mutha-fucker. I got up and looked out the window at the barn. It reminded me of my parent's place. My old room had been facing the barn as well. A memory came to mind as I stood there looking out.

It was storming that night at the house. My father was outside trying to put up a couple of horses. I had a solid black horse called Farrow. He was a pretty tall stud. I watched my father try to restrain Farrow, but he kept bucking because of the rain and lightning. I grabbed my rain coat, and I headed out to help him. As I approached the front door, my mama stood there, blocking me.

"Where are you going?' she asked with this evil look.

"Father needs help," I responded.

"Well, you won't be helping him today," she replied as she shoved my head backwards and I fell to the hard wood floor. I sat

70

there looking at her. She was so evil to me. She opened the front door, and looked out at him. She slammed the door shut and said, "He doesn't need you. I am his wife, not you. Stay in your place, little girl." She gave me a kick on the bottom of my rain boot. That memory disappeared as I heard the house pop. I lay back down and tried to rest. As I looked up at the chipped paint on the ceiling I thought about Vanessa. I guess I shouldn't be mad at her, because she had been through just as much as I had, but I couldn't help it.

It's sad that we are sisters and can't stand one another. I remember we had an argument over who Father loved the most. She thought he loved her more because they spent a lot of nights together, but I knew different. Father loved me more because he was very gentle with me, and not her. He was rough with Vanessa; I had seen it myself. She hated me, and I hated her, because we were fighting for our father's love. She was Mama's baby girl. Mama gave her the world and I was stuck in it. In the back of my mind, I would always wonder why a mother would love one child and not the other.

Vanessa had to know that Father was molesting her and making love to me; but she probably didn't give a damn. It was true that he spent more time with Vanessa, but he loved me more. I turned over, and closed my eyes. I had to get some rest for tomorrow; why were all these memories coming back now?

Chapter 9

The sun poured into the bedroom window, and I jumped up looking around. I leaped to my feet, and ran outside. I looked around like I had lost my mind; it seemed like everything was going in circles. My head started spinning, so I sat down on the ground, holding my head.

It seemed like I was hearing clicking noises in my head. I swayed my head from side to side. Nicole was trying to slip back in, but that bitch was gone.

I got off the ground, and went back inside the house to get my keys and leave. I was going to visit my mother. It wouldn't be right if I didn't talk to her; there were so many questions I needed to ask her, and I needed answers. Today was Saturday, and she doesn't work. Plus Vanessa was home too. I needed her there as well. They were going to talk to me today, or else. Fuck ignoring the problem anymore. My pain wasn't going away until I had answers. Those two females were the ones who could relieve me of this; I have feelings just like they do.

My mother lived out in the country, away from the city of Seattle, in a small place called Newcastle. Many people knew of me there; I'd lived there all my life until I decided to move to Vegas. Since I'm twenty-four years old now, and have picked up a

few pounds, they probably have forgotten about me or wouldn't recognize me.

I drove about two hours before I got to Newcastle. I pulled into my mother's driveway, and saw Vanessa's car parked outside. Mom's car must have been inside the garage. I parked, put the 9 mm in my back, and got out. My house key was still on the key ring, so I let myself in. I opened the door to the smell of nothing but sweet maple bacon. I walked into the kitchen, and my mom was over the stove looking like she was stirring up grits. I just stood there watching her; she didn't even hear me come in. Hurt and anger filled my heart. Something wanted me to break down and cry to her, but she was a mean bitch. I didn't want to be weak in front of her, because she would definitely make fun of me as she always did.

"Hello Mama," I said.

"Oh Lord, Nicole! You scared me," she replied while grabbing her chest.

"Mama, I asked you not to call me that. My name is Nikki," I responded.

"Well, I named you, so I will call you whatever I want," she retorted.

"I wouldn't do that if I was you," I whispered to myself.

"What the hell you say?" she asked in a louder voice.

"Nothing Mama. Where's Vanessa?" I asked.

"In her room sleep; go and wake her up for breakfast. Are you hungry? You look like you could use a good meal," she sarcastically said.

I didn't respond to her, but proceeded down the hall to wake up Vanessa. I grabbed the door handle, and just opened it; she was kneeling beside the bed praying.

"Breakfast is ready," I interrupted and slammed the door behind me. She probably thought I was a real bitch, but I didn't give a fuck.

We all sat quietly at the table. Until...

"Nicole, why are you here. Are you broke?" Mama blurted out.

"Stop calling me that. Call me Nikki or call me nothing," I shot back.

"Okay Nothing, why are you here?" Mama snapped.

"Mama, don't do that," Vanessa interrupted with a little fear in her face.

"Leave her alone Vanessa. Let your mama say whatever she wants to," I interjected.

"I'm your mama too, girl; and don't you forget it!" she yelled while throwing hot grits into my lap. That shit burned right through my pants.

"Shit, are you out your fucking mind?!" I yelled out as I jumped up.

"You are out of line!" Mama yelled.

"Bitch, I will fuck you up. I will kill your ass and feed you to the mutha-fucking dogs you have outside!" I yelled back.

"Your ass needs to stop cursing me in my own house. You will respect me," she said.

"Respect you? Bitch, I stopped respecting you when you starting fucking me. A mother is supposed to love her children, not fuck them," I lashed out at her.

I got up, trying to shake the hot grits off my pants. Vanessa ran over and brought me a towel. She began to help wipe me off, but I snatched the towel away. She immediately backed off, as I gave her that *don't fuck with me* look.

"Do you really hate me that much, old lady?" I asked.

"You are a bastard child. I should have never had you because you are evil," she said.

"Evil? Bitch you are evil. How can you let grown ass men rape your twelve-year-old daughter?!" I yelled.

"Rape? I was told you invited them into your room," she replied.

"Invited? Is that what you told her Vanessa?" I directed the question at her while looking directly into her eyes.

"Nicole, I mean Nikki, it wasn't like that. How did I know they were going to rape you?" she answered.

I started kicking over chairs and yelled, "Bitch, you were fucking high! Did you tell your mama you were too high to protect me? Did you?"

"Nicole. I was..." Vanessa stuttered.

"Bitch, don't stutter. Did your mama tell you how she was fucking me when I was younger? My bad, she was fucking you too. How can a mother fuck her own kids? We are fucking females!" I yelled.

Mama held her head down with her eyes closed.

"Bitch, hold your fucking head up. Do you have anything to say for yourself, or are you just going to hang your head low? All those nights you fondled and fucked me. Did you think I would forget that shit? Bitch, you were wrong for fucking your own kids. Don't be ashamed now," I continued.

Mama looked at Vanessa, but didn't say a word. Mama was about to walk out, when I pulled the 9 mm from my back. "Stop old lady, or I will kill you," I warned.

"Oh Lord," Vanessa cried out.

"Don't cry now, bitch! You hate me, remember?" I taunted.

"Nicole," Mama called out. I walked over to her and put the gun directly between her eyes and spoke clearly. "If you call me Nicole again, I will pull this fucking trigger."

Vanessa began to cry like the pussy she was. "Both of you get on your knees right beside each other. I have some questions to ask," I said.

They both kneeled slowly while looking at each other.

"You two bitches look so pathetic. Question number one is for you, Mother. Why did you fail to help me?" I asked. She began to open her mouth, and I interrupted, "No, no, no, don't answer that. I forgot, you thought I invited them to fuck me," I said dryly.

Looking over to Vanessa, I said, "Question number two. Why did you not help me? I'm your fucking sister." She didn't say a word, but cried more tears. "My bad Vanessa; are you scared? My big gun scaring you?" I asked. Before she could say a word, I released a bullet into her shoulder. *Pow!* The bitch fell backwards.

"Oh Lord, what are you doing?" Mama yelled, as Vanessa's body hit the ground.

"If you help her, the next bullet will be for you. Right between your fucking eyes," I threatened.

Vanessa lay on the floor, as blood oozed out. She began to cry out louder and louder for Mama to help her. Tears fell down Mama's face, but she didn't move. I got up and walked over to Vanessa. "Stop yelling; I won't ask you again," I stated as I kicked her in her stomach over and over and over again. My mind went blank, and I just kept kicking her until blood flowed from her mouth, nose, and ears.

"Leave her alone!" Mama yelled.

I walked around Vanessa's body to get to her, and tapped that mutha-fucker in the face with the gun. Her body fell backwards, landing next to Vanessa's. I began kicking her too, over and over again. After I finished, she lay there looking stupid

in the face, trying to gather herself. Vanessa looked over at Mama, while more tears poured down her face.

"Question number three, Mother: Did you ever love me?" I asked.

I waited for her to answer my question; there was silence in the room. While I looked into her eyes as I stood over her, I could only see hate—just like Marvin.

She slowly spoke, "Yes, of course I did."

"Say it. Tell me that you love me. Never mind, don't say a word. You just lay there," I stated as I picked up the house phone and dialed my friend Jake. Jake had just gotten out of jail and was looking for his next victim. He had been to prison for fifteen years for raping and sodomizing a woman. He had a few screws loose, but the court said he was sane enough to stand trial.

"Hello," a deep voice answered the phone.

"May I speak to Jake," I asked.

"This me. Who this?" he asked.

"Nigga, this Nikki from over on Lakewood. Across the river," I answered.

"Damn girl, I haven't heard from you in so long; but I do thank you for the letters and shit you sent to me while I was in the joint," he responded.

"Anytime, Nigga; I have a job for you. Do you think you can swing through?" I whispered.

"What kind of job you got for me?" he asked.

"What you get in trouble for Nigga? I got two right now. Come on over across the river," I demanded.

"Oh hell yeah, but I'm not trying to go back to prison," he said nervously.

"Nigga, I got you. You just hurry your ass up before I give the job to someone else," I urged.

"Hell naw, Nikki. I'm on my way," he said and hung up the phone in my face.

I hung up the phone and looked at them two as they lay on the floor with blood running from them. I sat at the kitchen table and shook my head. I wanted to go ahead and kill these two mutha-fuckers. They had caused enough problems in my life; but I would end this shit today. I didn't give a fuck about family; family had never been there for me before.

As I sat there waiting for Jake to arrive, my thoughts went back to when Father came into my room one night. It seemed like I could still smell him all over the house, even now. I remembered lying in the bed as he walked through the door. He walked over to me and pulled the covers back; we would always play this game called ride the horsy. I got up out of bed and walked with Father over to this chair. He took off my pajamas and told me to sit on him. There were so many times that I wanted to scream for Mama. I knew Father wouldn't hurt me, but the stuff he did at times really hurt. That night I didn't want to, but I knew he loved me so much, so I would have done anything Father asked me to

do. Before I got on top of him, he would put some type of clear jelly stuff on my pussy. As I got older, I learned it was KY Jelly.

He would motion his finger in and out of me, until I was ready. He would always ask me if I was ready; I would nod my head, and he would motion for me to straddle him. He would penetrate me slowly until I got used to him, and then would buck me up and down like I was riding a real horse. Before he would shoot off, he would lift me in the air and use his hand to do the rest. I would stand there and watch him. As that thought ran across my mind, I looked over at Mama.

"Get up on your knees, Mama. I have something to say and I want to make damn sure that you're listening," I said. She slowly got up off the floor with this scared look on her face. She braced herself up on her knees.

"Did you know that Father was fucking me and Vanessa? You two were fucking your own kids. How sick is that? He used to sneak in my room just like you, and take me like a grown ass woman. I know he fucked Vanessa on the regular, and you didn't say a word. Not a word Mama," I ranted.

She just sat there looking down at the floor. I couldn't believe that this bitch knew her husband was fucking her daughters, and she didn't do a damn thing to stop him. What the fuck was really going on? I sat there just staring at her, hoping she would defend herself; say she was sorry or something. She just sat there on her knees, like I wasn't even talking to her. I jumped up and ran over to her. As soon as I reached her, I kicked her in her fucking chest, sending her body flying backwards a few feet. She let out a loud cry, and Vanessa covered her eyes. This was some

fucked up shit, and my mama didn't give a fuck. Well, I was not going to have mercy on her today.

I began to walk over to her, when I heard a car pull up. I ran over to the window and looked out; I saw Jake and some other nigga jumping out of a car. "What the hell is he doing?" I asked myself as I made my way to the front door and swung it open.

"What the fuck, Jake? I thought you were coming by yourself," I said.

"I was, but Chris wanted a piece of the action too," Jake explained.
"Who the fuck is Chris?" I asked while checking dude out from head to toe.

"Me and Chris got out the joint at the same time; he's good people. Now where them hunnies at, Nikki?" he asked.

"Mama and Vanessa are on the inside. Be careful because they have a little blood on them," I replied.

"Blood? Bitch, are you crazy?" Jake yelled out.

"Nigga, just fuck and get it over with. I will handle the rest," I said.

"Yo' mama? I can't fuck her," he stated.

"Well, let this Chris dude fuck Mama and you fuck Vanessa. You know you want her; you've been trying to fuck her for years," I replied.

Jake rushed up to the door and Chris followed. I really wasn't feeling this Chris nigga. As soon as they finished; I would kill him too. I might kill Jake, but he's no snitch. They walked in the house and found my mother and sister on the floor.

"Which one I'm gonna get?" Chris asked.

I pointed, "You're fucking that old bitch over there," I said.

He ran over there and began ripping off clothes. Jake dragged Vanessa out in the open. She began yelling and screaming. I walked over and put the gun in her face. "Bitch, you will die if you yell out again," I threatened.

Vanessa had on pajamas and a shirt. Jake tore off her clothes too, and began fucking immediately. He was ramming, and ramming Vanessa hard. I got me a chair and looked while I ate a little more breakfast. I could hear Mama over there moaning; she deserved every bit of this punishment. Chris turned her over and she yelled out over and over, as he rammed her ass. Jake made Vanessa suck his dick while she bled out. I guess she was slow, so he shoved her back down onto the floor. He flipped her over and began fucking her in the ass too. They both were pounding away; all you could hear was dick slapping against ass, and screams.

I got up and walked back to my room as those two nuts fucked. Chris was choking Mama down as he fucked; he was rougher than Jake. The only thing running across my mind was would those two assholes snitch. I wasn't too worried about Jake though, because we grew up together.

I walked up to my bedroom door, but I couldn't go in. Another memory crossed my mind of when I'd come out my room

once and heard Vanessa cry out. I walked over to her door, and peeped through this small crack. I could see father ramming her hard; he was gentler with me. I sat there and stared, until Vanessa looked toward the door with tears running down her face. We made eye contact, and I jumped back. I didn't want Father to see me, because he would probably come to my room; and I didn't want him to. I had placed my hand on the door knob, when I heard Jake scream out. I ran back up the hall, only to see that he had came all over Vanessa's face. I looked over at Chris; he was still going and going and going.

Jake stood up with his dick in his hand, still stroking. "How many times can I fuck?" he asked me.

"Nigga, I don't have all night to wait on you two," I replied.

"Man, I wanted to get another nut. Her ass was tighter than I thought," he said wistfully, while looking down at Vanessa.

"Well, go ahead and get another nut, but I have to go soon. I have shit I need to do," I responded.

"Nikki, you know I got you. Just go ahead and do whatever you have to do. Me and Chris will be here until you get back. I want to fuck until I pass the fuck out. You know we fresh out the joint," Jake said.

"Hell yeah. I like this pussy; I can fuck all night," Chris said with a slow slang.

"Hell yeah, Nigga!" Jake yelled out.

"You two niggas finish fucking then, and I will be back. After you get through, tie them up and don't go anywhere. Jake, I'm trusting you," I replied.

"Nikki, have I ever failed you before?" he asked.

"No, you haven't, but make sure things are straight. I will be right back," I said as I began to walk out the door. I looked back before I closed the door and saw Jake jump on top of Vanessa. He began pounding away. Vanessa and I made eye contact; I just shook my head and slammed the front door.

As I got in my car, I didn't know whether I should leave or wait until those two fools finished.

"Bitch, are you sure you want to leave them two here? They could fuck and then snitch on your black ass," Nikki spoke.

"Jake won't tell. I don't know about that Chris guy though," I said.

"You are fucking up already; you leaving evidence, and now witnesses. What the fuck are you doing?" Nikki asked.

"Let me handle this Nikki. You just sit your ass back and let me handle all this," I responded.

I cranked the car and drove off. I didn't know where I was going. I looked back at the house, and I just hit the gas, spinning wheels. The only reason why I was leaving was because I didn't want to hear any more of their cries. I'd cried for years and nobody helped me.

Chapter 10

As I drove down the highway, I decided to ride by Kevin's mama house. His mama had an old run-down white house with black shutters. He was one of the men who'd raped me. It was a day I would never forget, and I would never forget his ugly ass face. He had a scar going down the right side of his face where he was kicked by one of his horses. The mutha-fucker should have killed him, but it was okay; he would get what he deserved.

Damn, this was my lucky day, because that punk was there standing outside. I began to feel all warm inside because I was taking that nigga out today, before I went back to Vegas. I continued to ride on, because a car was pulling into the driveway. As the old red Chevy Cavalier pulled in, I saw Keith and James inside. My head started banging, and so much hurt filled my heart. Bits and pieces of the rape played over and over in my head. I turned away from them, looking straight ahead; but not before James and I looked into each other's eyes. He knew exactly who I was. There was no way any of them would ever forget my face. It had been a long time, but to me, it felt like all of this had happened yesterday.

I drove on down the street until I was out of sight. I pulled my car to the side, popped my trunk, and got out the Air Force

Talon SS. Then I took some ammo and loaded that bitch. She was locked and ready to bust some ass. I put the high power rifle on the passenger seat, turned the car around and proceeded back to Kevin's mama house. The rape played over and over in my head; the images of me screaming, telling them to stop as they kept fucking me. Nobody heard my cry. Well today, nobody would hear their cries.

As I pulled up in the driveway, I noticed Keith and James were still sitting on the inside of the car, while Kevin stood outside. The expression on Kevin's face as he turned and saw me, told me that he knew who I was. I put the car in park, and pulled out my bitch. As I opened the car door, Kevin noticed my gun and began to run. I jumped out like Rambo and cut that bitch down to pieces. His body fell to the ground, and I began to spray that red Cavalier with bullets. Bodies were jerking and bouncing as bullets tore at their skin. Kevin moved and I turned on him and sprayed that ass some more. His body jerked a couple of times and that was it. To make sure there weren't any witnesses, I began to shoot up that fucking house. It didn't matter to me who was inside that mutha-fucker. The gun ran out of bullets, so I walked back to the trunk of my car, reloaded and continued to shoot up the house and the red Cavalier. This time after I ran out of bullets, I walked over to the car and looked in. Their faces were gone; bodies just limp. The doors to the car fell off.

I heard a loud crash, and saw pieces of the roof cave in. I walked slowly over to Kevin, and turned him over. He had no face, just blood running out of his head. A big ass fucking hole. I started walking away from him, then I ran back and kicked him in the face and spit on him. I kicked and kicked and kicked him until I was out

of breath. After that, I decided to take off my pants and thong and do one last thing. I slid one leg out and bent down to piss on his faceless body. After I finished pissing in what used to be his face, I pulled up my clothes and stared at him for a few seconds. I could still see the rape so clearly. I lay helplessly on the floor, as they took my tiny body and tortured me. They all had man-sized dicks that they'd just shoved inside of me. Tears fell down my face as screams rang from my mouth. It hurt me, because it had been a long time since I had been penetrated like that. My father had done it all the time, but he was slow. He didn't hurt me like those fools did. When my mama did it with her finger; I didn't say anything. If I had; I would've gotten beat like no tomorrow.

Suddenly, I snapped out of my memory as more pieces of the roof collapsed. I shook my head, and headed back to my car. I looked over at Keith and James; fuck them all. I didn't give a damn.

I put my Air Force Talon SS on the passenger seat and was headed back to Vegas, then I thought about it. I had to go back home and burn those fucking bodies. I just prayed that the police were not there with Jake and Chris. Then again, them two niggas didn't want to go back to jail. Fuck it, I was turning around. I had to burn those bodies; I had to take that chance. I really didn't give a fuck if I got caught or not. *Fuck the police.*

Chapter 11

As I drove back to the house, all types of thoughts ran through my mind. I was thinking that these two fools may have called the police and snitched on me. I could see police all over the place in my imagination, but when I arrived, it was nearly dark and the yard was empty. The sun was about to go down, and as I pulled up, I didn't see Jake's car nowhere. That bitch was gone. The front door was cracked open; I jumped out of the car and ran up the steps. When I pushed the door open, I saw Mama and Vanessa hugged up with each other, bleeding. Blood was all over the place. I didn't know what the hell had went on. I walked over and looked down at the two; Vanessa's eyes popped open. She gave Mama a nudge, and one of her eyes popped open. The other eye was closed shut. They both looked like somebody had beaten the shit out of them.

"Damn, I thought you two bitches were dead," I said, as I walked back to the front door and closed it. I walked through the house looking, but I saw no signs of Jake or Chris. Those two fools had fucked and ran off. Now suppose one of my relatives had been strong enough to get some help? I looked over at the phone, and saw the cord was snatched away from the wall. At least somebody had enough sense to do that. I'd told that mutha-

fucking Jake to stick around, but I guess he said he didn't want any part of this anymore. I picked up a chair, sat down in it, and looked at the two of them, as they stared back at me.

"Now Mama, where were we again? I asked you question number one and question number two; I guess we didn't get to finish question number three. My question was did you ever love me?" I asked again.

I sat there waiting for her to answer me. She moved away from Vanessa and sat up on the floor naked. I wanted to hear her answer. This bitch was about to lie, and I felt it.

She looked into my eyes, swallowed, and said, "I love you Nicole."

"Wrong answer," I replied, then pulled the trigger and shot her right between the eyes. Her body fell to the floor next to Vanessa. Vanessa began screaming, so I pointed and shot her in the face too. I rose from the chair, and began jumping up and down.

"Nikki, what have you done?!" I screamed. Tears fell down my face while I screamed. Finally, I stopped and with no remorse, Nikki replied, "something you always wanted to do." I walked over and poured more bullets into their bodies, making sure they were dead. I continued to shoot until the 9 mm ratcheted back, letting me know no more bullets were chambered in the gun.

I walked over to the sink, placed the gun on the marble counter, and turned on the water to wash my face off. I looked out the small window and noticed the grass was dead. When my father lived; he took care of all of this. My mama was an evil bitch

that didn't deserve a good burial like my father. She was just like the men I dated; she liked to use people.

After washing off, I fixed a sandwich and began eating. Looking at Mama and Vanessa lying dead on the floor gave me a big happy feeling and I smiled. They never loved me; in all my twenty-four years of living, they had shown nothing but hate. Family just wasn't the same anymore.

After I finished eating my sandwich and drinking my coke, I washed my plate and put it in the rack. Looking over at Mama, I said, "Well Mama, I finished my plate this time. You have always beaten me if I didn't finish. This time, I did what you asked me to do."

I stepped over Vanessa and proceeded down the hall to my old bedroom. I stood at the door, hesitating to go in. Finally, I got up the nerve, and opened the door. There was no bed, no dressers, no pictures on the wall, and nothing in the closet. The room was empty. My mama had gotten rid of everything that reminded her of me. I just slammed the door shut and walked back down the hall.

I walked back over to the refrigerator, took another piece of cheese, and put it in my mouth. I looked at the two of them laid out on the floor and smiled. Then I began to laugh out loud. I put the gun in my back, and walked over to the front door. I looked back and said, "Bye Mama. Bye Vanessa. I have given you two what you have shown me all these years. Nothing." I walked out and slammed the door. I stood there for a few minutes, thinking maybe I should burn their bodies or cut those bitches up and feed them to the fucking mutts running around.

I continued to walk on towards the car. After sitting in the car for a few minutes looking into the rear view mirror at Nikki, I decided to burn the bodies in the barn. It would have been crazy for me to come all the way back over here, and not burn them; that's what my intentions were.

I walked back inside the house; I grabbed Vanessa's body and slowly pulled her to the end of the steps. She was a little heavy, so I went in the house and grabbed one of Daddy's old belts. Putting it around her neck, I began dragging her down the steps until her body hit the ground. I dragged and dragged until I was tired. I rested for a few minutes, then continued on. After placing her body in the barn, I went back and dragged Mama out the same way—by her neck. It seemed like it was easier that way.

After I placed the bodies in the barn, I gathered gas from the shed at the back of the house, and poured it everywhere. I poured gas all around and inside the house; poured gas inside and outside the barn, plus soaked the two bodies with gas, to make sure they would burn. I was sending those two bitches straight to hell. They would burn in hell for hurting me. I was so tired of being hurt. So, from that day forward, I would kill all of them that hurt me.

After soaking everything in gas, I drove to the end of the driveway. I poured a trail of gas that led back up to the house first, then the barn. I ran back down toward the driveway and lit the match. The fire ran back up so fast, and as soon as it hit the house, a big explosion sounded off. Windows busted out the house, then the barn let out a loud explosion. I stood there looking at this old ass place burn down. There would be no more

hurt, and no more pain on this land. All the terrible memories were cleansed from here, but not from my mind.

"Bitch, you need to hurry up and leave," Nikki interrupted my thoughts.

"Nobody is coming all the way out here," I said.

"You never know. Where are Jake and Chris? Those two could be setting you up right mutha-fucking now with the cops, or maybe the Feds. Bitch, lets get out of here," she urged.

"You right. You've gotten us in enough hot water," I said.

"Bitch, this is all you killing. Don't you love the taste of blood?" she asked.

I replied, "Yeah. Revenge is so sweet."

Chapter 12

Crossing the Nevada state line felt so damn good. My business was finished back home. People probably would think I'm sick for killing all those fuckers for hurting me. Fuck them all. This is all about me: *Nikki*.

I was driving and shit, and had completely forgotten about the Air Force Talon SS that was still sitting in the passenger seat. What the fuck was I thinking? I pulled to the side of the street, and carefully wrapped and put it away with the others. As I got back on the road, my thoughts were of my mama.

At the age of ten, how could anyone blame a child? My father had been sick for about a year; the doctors had diagnosed him with lung cancer. From that day forward, my father and I became like two peas in a pod. I had always been Daddy's little girl. Even though my father did some crazy stuff to me, he was gentle, and I appreciated and loved him more for that. I loved my daddy and he could do nothing wrong in my eyes. Mama always made him out to be a monster. I guess she was upset, because he spent more time with me than her. He didn't molest me all the time; only sometimes when Vanessa wasn't there. A few times, he would go to Vanessa late at night. It made me wonder when he ever had time for Mama, because it seemed like he was always with us. It doesn't matter what my father did; I will always love

him more. At the time, I thought it was right for me to fuck my father; but as I got older, I realized it was wrong. Vanessa was getting screwed more than me but Father loved me more. People used to say that I looked just like him, and my mother couldn't stand that shit. She hated anyone who thought that.

I can remember the day my father died. We had come back from the doctor's office, and he seemed so distant. In my mind, I think he knew he was going to die that day. My mother was at work like always, and Vanessa had gone over to her friend's Janet house to study.

My father lay down on his bed and looked up at the ceiling.

"Father, what's wrong with you?" I asked him, while sitting on the bed next to him.

"Baby girl, I don't think I can hold on anymore," he spoke slowly.

"What do you mean, Father?" I asked.

"Well, it's time for me to go heaven," he replied.

"No Father, I'm not ready for you to go. Please don't leave me," I begged.

"Don't cry, baby girl. Remember we talked about this day," he reminded me.

"Yes, but it's not today. I don't want you to leave me. I'm not ready," I pleaded.

"If you leave me, Mama will treat me wrong. Please don't let her," I continued.

"She loves you baby girl, and you know this," Father said.

"She beats me when you aren't around. She cusses me out and hits me in the face. Father, please don't leave me alone with her," I pleaded.

For the first time, I saw tears fall down my father's face as he spoke, "I pray the Lord will keep me around longer to protect you. I'm so sorry baby girl, for your mother's actions. I didn't know how often she was treating you like that," my father said.

"Father please, what can I do to help you get better?" I asked.

He grabbed my head and I placed it on his chest. He rubbed my hair while humming to me. He began coughing hard, so I sat up and tried to help him.

"You know I love you," he said.

"I love you too Father," I replied.

"I need some water baby girl," he said.

I ran out to the kitchen to get a glass of water. I ran back to the bedroom with the water, and as I stepped in the door, I saw my father looking up toward the sky. He looked at me then back up toward the sky, and tears fell down his face again. I dropped the glass of water, and ran over to the bed. As I sat on the bed, I looked into his face. He gasped for air twice, and then stopped breathing. His last breath was deep. As I sat there and watched my father die, so much hurt and anger filled my heart. *What was God thinking? He was supposed to take bad people like my mother, not an angel like my father. What was I going to do without him? Who would protect me from all this pain?* I thought.

Instead of calling the ambulance or my mother, I sat there next to my dad all day long. I then lay next to him as his body became stiff. I knew he was dead, but what could I do? When my mother came home and saw my father dead, she screamed and screamed. I had fallen asleep and she woke me up screaming. She scared me so bad, I pissed on myself. As I stood there, pee ran down my legs onto the wooden floor.

"What have you done?" she screamed at me.

"Nothing Mama," I responded.
"Your father is dead. You killed him!" she yelled as she slapped me across the face. I fell to the ground crying, looking up at her. She continued, "You little bitch, you killed him!"

"No Mama, please don't hurt me!" I screamed out to her. She grabbed my father's black leather belt off the wall and began beating me like I was nothing to her. The black belt had holes, so as she beat me, she left circle marks all over me.

At that moment, I knew she hated me. My mama beat me so bad I couldn't move. She didn't stop until Vanessa came home and stopped her. If it wasn't for Vanessa, I probably would have died right there with my father. That woman was evil and she wondered where I got it from. I hated the day my father died and left me with that evil ass woman. I'm so fucking glad she's dead. I'm glad I burned her body; I should have flushed the ashes down the toilet. That evil bitch ruined my childhood. After Vanessa's friends raped me, she locked me in my room like a slave. I only came out when I had to go to school. I blamed Vanessa, because she didn't help me. She didn't protect me like she promised. Both those bitches can rot in hell...

Chapter 13

Finally, I made it back home. I walked into my apartment, and it seemed like I hadn't been there in forever. As I walked in farther, I could hear someone moving around. I took out the 9 mm and walked into the living room.

"What the fuck are you doing here?" I asked Jeremy. I continued, "How in the hell did you get in here?"

"Remember, you gave me a key?" he asked.

"Well, what do you want? Why in the hell are you here?" I repeated.

"You asked me that already," he stated.

"Well?" I asked.

"Did you burn Dena's house down?" he asked.

"What the fuck? Why you accusing me nigga?" I angrily replied.

"Because shit has been happening to me that I can't explain, and you seem to be the only one I can blame. Plus, Derek told me to watch your crazy ass," he explained.

"Derek. Are you serious?" I asked.

"I'm keeping my eye on you. I believe you're trying to fuck my world up, but that shit will never happen," he said as he stood up.

"Boy, get the fuck out of my apartment talking stupid. Why in the hell would I want to hurt you?" I asked.

"Not me, but the women in my life," he said.

I just stood there looking at him. There was nothing I could say about that. He was right; I wanted all those bitches dead. If he wasn't going to love me, then they weren't going to love him. Jeremy walked over to me and said, "Nicole, Nikki; whoever the fuck you are. Stay the fuck out of my life."

"You can call me Nikki. You are a weak bitch. How can you believe Derek, of all people? I have always been there for you," I said.

"Yes, I know. That's what I'm afraid of," he answered.

We stood there looking down at the floor. I walked up to him to kiss him, and he shoved me backward. "What the fuck are you doing?" he asked.

I laid the 9 mm down on the counter, because he kept watching it. "Where in the hell did you get that gun?" Jeremy asked.

"It was my father's; I got it from home," I lied.

"You've been home?" He asked.

"Yes. How could I do anything if I was in Washington? Get real," I replied.

"You have a valid point," he replied as he started to think clearly.

We stood there a few minutes more, and then he rushed me. He put his tongue down my throat, kissing me passionately. My man had finally given in; he really wanted me. Jeremy began to take off his clothes. I began rushing to take off mine. We were staring at each other, rushing to get undressed. He ran back up to me biting me on my breasts; I loved that pain. Both his hands caressed me hard. I reached down below, touching his cock and making it harder and harder for me.

Suddenly, he turned me around and bent me over. My pussy was wet and ready to be fucked. He entered me abundantly, and I pushed back on his cock roughly. We both were banging and banging away at each other. He grabbed me by my shoulders, forcing himself deeper and deeper. "Oh Jeremy," I moaned.

"Call my name," he panted.

"Jeremy. Jeremy. Jeremy." I repeated over and over.

As I yelled out his name; he got faster and faster. Then his cum came out in loads. He busted right there; I jumped down on my knees while he busted all over my face. I knew my king was saving that nut for me.

After our fuck session, he pulled up his pants and walked over to the door. He looked back, staring at me. He looked as if he wanted to say something, but didn't. He just walked out, leaving

me with a wet pussy—again. I laid on the floor, and curled up into a ball. I hummed to myself, as I thought of us getting married. I could see Jeremy getting down on his knees, asking me to marry him. As I lay with beautiful thoughts of us on my mind, the killings invaded my thoughts. I could hear all the screams and cries for help. The ones that rang out the loudest were the cries of my mama, and I began to cry. Tears ran down my face as I called out to my father. Images of him appeared before me. They were so real, I sat up, reaching out to my father.

He said to me, "Baby girl, what are you doing? I love you so much and I wish that I were there for you. Please stop all this madness."

"Father, she hurt me. You promised to protect me. Why did you have to leave me?" I cried.

"Baby girl, I'm sorry I'm not around to protect you from all the hurt and all the pain you are experiencing; but you have to remember that God loves you. I love you," he said.

"I love you Father. I need you here to hold me. The hurt is so deep and I don't know how to stop all this," I said.

"You're hurting innocent people. Baby girl, stop this madness. If not for me, then do it for yourself. I know you are suffering from pain and grief, but you can't blame everyone for it. Everything is going to be okay. I wish I could hold you tight and protect you, but I'm far away," he said.

"I can be far away like you. I want to go with you, Father. Father, please," I begged.

"When God is ready, he will call you home to join us. Until then, remember that you will always be my baby heart. I will always love you," he said.

"Father, I need you. Please don't leave me," I pleaded as the images disappeared.

My body went limp, and I fell to the floor. I began crying out louder and louder. It hurt me so bad that I'd lost the one true person who loved me: my father.

Chapter 14

This is a new day and I'm going to spend time with Jeremy. He said he wants me to come over to his house. I took a long bath, put on my *Love Spell* body splash by Victoria's Secret, and put on my yellow flowered sundress. This was the day I had been dreaming about. This nigga had finally come to his senses. As I packed my 9 mm into my purse, the thoughts of him pissing me off ran through my mind. He loved to surprise me with some stupid shit. Some bullshit that would set me off; but I felt like today was going to be totally different. He sounded so happy over the phone.

I arrived fifteen minutes early, and there was a car in the driveway. It belonged to his friend Derek. What the hell is he doing over here? Probably feeding Jeremy all these lies about me. He's just upset because I won't fuck him. Well, maybe I should change my mind. Give him a little pussy and take him out the game, I thought to myself.

I rang the door bell, only to have Derek open the door.

"Well, if it isn't Little Miss Sunshine in the flesh," he mocked.

"Fuck you too Derek," I shot back.

"Bitch, you wish," he said.

This nigga was really trying to set me off. I walked past him and proceeded over to the bar where Jeremy sat.

"What's up girl?" he said.

"You told me to come over here," I replied.

"Yeah that's right. I almost forgot about that. I need a favor from you," he said.

Derek interrupted, "Man, stop fucking with this bitch. We all know that she wants you."

"Bitch?" I snapped.

"Oh my bad; crazy bitch," he said.

"Derek, man, stop fucking around," Jeremy interrupted.

"I'm so serious. This bitch is trying to set you up. Watch what I tell you," Derek warned.

"Why don't you just get the fuck out? Leave nigga. You might be setting him up, with your fake ass gold teeth stupid bitch self," I responded.

"Bitch, I'll fuck your whole world up," he threatened.

"Do it. Stop talking about it, and do it," I countered.

"Can you two get along for one minute?" Jeremy asked.

"Well, tell your boy to get off my thong," I replied.

"Bitch please," Derek spat out.

Jeremy grabbed me by the hand and took me down the hall. This wasn't going to turn out good, because we were headed to the bedroom. This was a first.

As we walked inside the bedroom, there was female stuff everywhere. I looked around the room, and my mind went nuts.

"What's all this bullshit?" I asked.

"That's Dena stuff. She didn't have a place to stay, so she's been here," Jeremy replied.

"Are you fucking serious?" I asked.

"Yes," he replied.

Jeremy continued talking, and I walked out. It seemed like my body was going in slow motion. I couldn't believe this pussy ass nigga had moved a bitch in with him. There was no way I was going to let this shit ride.

"Where the fuck you going girl?" Jeremy asked while following me down the hall.

"Looks like the bitch is leaving," Derek mocked.

I gave him this look and walked out the door. Jeremy came to the door, looking at me as if he was puzzled. Derek ran out behind him talking shit. "Bye bitch," he waved.

"Nicole, hold up," Jeremy said as he ran behind me. Before I could close the car door he grabbed it, and swung it back open.

"What the fuck do you want? Don't you have a woman that can do you favors?" I asked.

"I'm asking you, not her. I trust you, not her," he replied.

"Why don't you trust a bitch that's living in the house with you?" I asked.

"What's your problem?" he asked.

"My problem is when you make stupid ass decisions like this. Do you know anything about this girl?" I questioned.

"Can I ask you the favor?" he continued on, like nothing was wrong.

"Bitch, no. Get the fuck out my door," I snapped, as I pulled my door up and shut it. Derek yelled out again, "Bye crazy bitch!"

I started burning rubber, and drove off; I took the 9 mm out of my purse and laid it on the seat.

"Go back and kill that bitch. Go back! Go back!" I yelled to myself.

Fuck it. I turned the mutha-fucking car around and went back. As I headed back towards his house I saw Dena pulling into the driveway. Derek and Jeremy were still standing outside. I looked both those bitches in the face and pointed my 9 mm toward the house. They both ducked. I'm coming back; you best to believe I will be back.

Chapter 15

A couple of weeks passed by, and I felt so deranged. The thought of another woman in Jeremy's bed every night was too much. Fuck it; Dena had to die tonight.

I rode past her job, and parked my car in a dark alley. She worked the late night shift at IHOP on Highway 468. I watched as she got in her car and drove. I looked in my rearview mirror to see if anyone was following us. She was driving kind of slow, and it looked like she was talking on a cell phone. I looked down at my Louisville slugger baseball bat; tonight was the night.

We stopped at a red light and I ran into the back of her car. I sat there for a few seconds and she jumped out.

"Bitch, you hit my car!" she screamed as she came towards me. I looked around to see if anyone had spotted us. I let down the window and said, "Ma'am, I'm so sorry."

"Bitch, I hope you have insurance," she continued to say while walking up to the car.

I stepped out of the car as she walked up, and said to her, "Ma'am, I'm so sorry."

"Sorry? Bitch do you have insurance?" she asked.

"Yes I do, but I really wish you'd stop calling me that," I said to her.

"You just hit me from the back, and you think I'm supposed to be your mutha-fucking friend? Bitch, I'm calling the police," she replied.

"Hold on. Let me make sure I have my card in the car before you call," I replied.

"What the fuck?" she said while pacing.

"Come with me over to the car," I said and she followed.

As I opened the car door, I reached in and pulled out my Louisville Slugger. She had her head turned, looking at her car shaking her head from side to side, talking cash money shit.

As I slammed the car door, she turned back to face me; that's when I took my baseball bat and knocked that bitch out. Blood and teeth flew from her mouth. I hit her so hard, it sounded like an egg cracking. She fell to the ground in slow motion; I just watched as she landed right in front of me. I kicked that whore right in her stomach, making her body jerk.

I jumped in my car and blew around her. I parked my car in a slot a little on down the street; I had to be fast before someone came by.

I ran back up to her car, and struggled to get that bitch in. She was out cold. After stuffing her in the back seat, I pulled her car down behind mine, jumped out and got into my own car. I had

to leave that bitch until I got back. I hoped she didn't get the fuck up.

As I left and headed to the gas station, a few cars passed by. Damn, I prayed no one stopped to help her. That would be my ass. This was the first time I'd left a victim alone. She probably wouldn't get up though; she had enough blood and teeth on the ground to prove she wasn't going to move.

I rushed to a store and got some gas. This time I made sure that I had gloves on. I'd made many mistakes by not doing so before. I was surprised the fucking Feds weren't looking for me.

I rushed back, but she was still in the back seat, out cold. I opened her sun roof, then locked the doors. I got on top of the car, and began pouring gas through the sunroof into the car. I made sure that her body was soaked with gas, and after that, I lit a match and tossed it into the car. The blaze caught up fast, so I quickly jumped down off the car. A few seconds passed by and I began to hear screams. At first I thought it was someone on the street, but they rang out from the car. Then I saw her.

Dena was screaming and screaming as she tried to get out. She stood up out the sunroof screaming for her life. All I could smell was flesh burning. Her burning skin had a charcoal like smell and her hair produced a sulfurous odor. It was a very unique smell that I really couldn't describe; but I liked it.

Suddenly, I saw car lights. I rushed back to my car and drove off. I looked back in the rearview mirror, and I didn't see her anymore. A smile came over my face, but it disappeared when I had a flash back. I remembered the day my pet rabbit was burned

alive. My father had bought me the rabbit; after he died, my mama got rid of everything I loved. That included my horse and my rabbit. I sat there while she burned my rabbit named Bonnie to a crisp. She made me sit there on the ground while the fire burned. She built a fire inside of an iron barrel, after she and Vanessa gathered plenty of wood to burn. She wanted me to be seated, and I didn't know what she was doing at the time.

After they finished gathering wood, Mama went to the barn and brought out the cage with Bonnie. I reached out my arms as if she was really going to give her to me. She looked at me with that evil eye, and I turned away like a scared child. She took Bonnie out the cage, held her up by the neck and said, "This rabbit will no longer be your pet. You don't need pets."

"But why Mama? I love her," I spoke softly.

She didn't reply back at all; she just snapped the rabbit's neck and tossed her in the fire. I jumped up and ran to the barrel, "No Mama. No!" I screamed.

Vanessa held me down on the ground while Bonnie burned. Mama was so cruel. I stopped squirming and fighting, and Mama walked over and dragged me back to the house by my hair. She locked me in my room for two days. Vanessa brought me food and water but that was it. That memory flashed away quick.

As I came back to reality, I felt good knowing that Dena was dead. Jeremy was mine. All mine.

Chapter 16

The following morning I sat at my table eating ice cream. I was waiting for my king to come home to me. Hours and hours passed by, and no Jeremy. I would have called him, but I didn't want to seem too anxious. Fuck it, I was going to call him anyway.

His phone just rang and rang and rang; he didn't pick up. I called him again, and still nothing. Suddenly, there was a soft knock at the door. I looked through the peep hole and saw Jeremy standing there. I opened the door for my king. Before I could get the door all the way open, he rushed in like a mad man, and forced me to the ground. He slammed the door, jumped down on me, and began punching me in the face and head.

"How could you kill her?" he yelled as he beat me.

"Jeremy please! Stop it!" I screamed.

I tried to fight back, but he was too strong. Thoughts raced through my head of when those boys had held me down and raped me. I couldn't defend myself; Jeremy stopped hitting me and began choking me. He squeezed and squeezed until I passed out.

I woke up to a dark room, and began to panic. I was looking and searching to see where I was.

"Don't move bitch," Jeremy said out of the darkness.

"Jeremy," I said.

"How could you kill Dena? What the fuck did she do so wrong to you?" he asked.

"What are you talking about? I didn't kill anyone! Turn on the fucking lights; I can't see," I said.

"Bitch, you don't need to see. You are so fucking evil," he retorted.

"Jeremy, please. You are talking outside your head," I said.

"Stop it Nikki; I know what you are. You don't think I fucking know you. I know you love me, and I know you're willing to kill for me. I don't want you," he said.

"But Jeremy—" I started.

"Don't 'but Jeremy' to me," he interrupted as he turned on the lights. I blinked my eyes, and tried to focus. As I looked into his face, it seemed like he had been crying. I had blood all over me. My left eye was halfway closed, and my body ached. Jeremy jumped up and ran over to me. He grabbed me by my hair and started dragging me into my other bedroom. I began kicking and holding my hair. He threw me into the room and said, "Look. I found all your guns and all your knives. What the fuck is wrong with you?!" He yelled.

"Jeremy, I love you so much," I said.

"Love? Bitch this ain't love. How? I don't fucking love you, and I definitely don't fucking want you anymore," he replied.

"You are confused right now," I said.

"Bitch, I'm not confused. My head is clear. You are one crazy mutha-fucker," he said.

"Explain why you don't want me?" I asked.

"Bitch, you are crazy. Look at this shit around you. You have guns and knives, and enough ammo to kill thousands of people. I can't be with you like this," he replied.

"I got all this when I went back home. Marvin and I had guns hidden, so I retrieved them and brought them back. I'm not a killer Jeremy," I explained.

"Then what are you? Nicole, I can't be with you anymore. Fuck this, I love my life," he said.

Before he could continue with all that bullshit, I rolled over and picked up my Air Soft Sniper Rifle. I pointed it at him, and that pussy ass nigga took off running down my hallway. You could hear him hitting the walls, and he was running like a wild man.

I jumped up and ran after him. I yelled, "Come back here, you little pussy! Tell me to my face now that you don't love me! Tell me now!"

He disappeared fast. He must have already had his escape planned just in case I escaped from him. I opened the door, but he was nowhere to be found. I locked my door and put down my rifle. I walked over to the balcony, and saw Jeremy jump in his car and spin tires as he left. He was running that Dodge Magnum wide open.

The first thing that hit my mind was to leave town. If I knew that weak bitch well; he would go to the cops with all this. I packed my shit and dipped. The heat was hot around Vegas, and there was no way I was going down. Not until I got my prize.

Chapter 17

I tossed and turned in my sleep. All I could think about was Jeremy. It had been two months, so I thought this shit would go away by now; but I was so in love. I sat up beside my bed, with sweat pouring down off my face. These nightmares had become so intense. This man had to become mine. I had killed so many just to be with the love of my life. Fuck that; I was going back to Vegas to get my man.

Things didn't seem the same because I wasn't living the city life. I'd found this small town called Iuka, Mississippi and made it my home. When I worked at the law firm, a client had sued the hospital from this city. It's a small country town and everyone knew everyone's business. There was this young man in Iuka named Timothy Buchannan, but everyone called him "Cowboy". He called himself being in love with me, but I didn't want him. I had a man back in Vegas. Cowboy was five eleven, weighed about two-hundred and fifty pounds, and had red hair. He was kind of a thick young buck with gray eyes; someone I could toy around with.

I sat at the sink drinking a glass of water, and looked out the window to see Cowboy sitting in my yard with his truck running. I waved and he waved back.

"What the fuck is he doing?" I asked myself.

I went outside to see what he wanted. It was around two o'clock in the morning. I walked up to his old Chevy pickup truck and asked, "What are you doing?"

"Well Nikki, I wanted to make sure that you were alright," he replied.

"At this time of morning? Nobody lives around here; I'm miles away from anyone," I said.

"Yeah, I know. You never know who's out here though," he responded in his country slang.

I thought to myself, bitch, you are the only dumb ass out this time of morning. Damn, is this fool stalking me? Even as I thought that, for some reason, he was starting to look good to me. I think it was the pussy beginning to talk.

"Would you like to come inside?" I asked.

"Oh yes ma'am," he excitedly said while jumping out of the truck.

"Maybe you should turn your truck off," I suggested.

Cowboy reached in and turned off the truck. He was staring at me like I was a piece of meat.

"That's a nice gown you have on there ma'am," he said.

"Thank you," I said.

I noticed that his cock was beginning to rise. He turned around the other way so I wouldn't notice. We began to walk back towards the house. The wind was blowing a little and my nipples

stuck up. As I opened the door, I stopped and bent over. Cowboy bumped into me with his hard cock right at my ass. If we didn't have any clothes on, his cock would have invaded my pussy.

"Oh Ms. Nikki, I'm so sorry about that," he apologized.

"That's okay Cowboy. Why is your cock so hard?" I asked.

He shied away like a little boy. This must have been his first time, or he wasn't getting any on a regular basis. As he had his head turned, I reached and felt his cock. He jumped like I had punched him.

"Calm down Cowboy. I'm not going to hurt you," I said.

He looked at me and stood up straight. I continued to rub him. He fell to his knees and came right there in his pants. I couldn't believe this shit. I had thought that this so called cowboy was going to give me a good fucking, but he came before he even touched my pussy.

"Are you alright?" I asked.

"I'm so sorry, Ms. Nikki. This is my third time being with a woman," he answered.

"Your third time?" I asked.

"Yes ma'am," he said.

"Stop calling me ma'am. Nikki or Ms. Nikki will do," I spoke harshly.

I grabbed him by the hair and pushed his head in my pussy. He began to sniff me like a dog. His hands came around grabbing

my ass. I put my leg up on his shoulder, and he licked me right there. He was like a hog eating slop. I turned around so he could eat my pussy from the back. He kept shoving his tongue deeper and deeper inside me. Finally, he got up off his knees and rammed his cock within me. He banged and banged like a mad man, and it actually felt good. My screams made him bang harder. It had become so intense that he slipped out and went straight in my ass.

"Damn!" I called out.

He acted as if he didn't hear anything. He grabbed me around the neck and pushed deeper in my ass.

"Stop it Cowboy. Stop it!" I yelled as he banged more. His grip was very tight. I began bucking and kicking. Finally, he loosened his grip, and I pushed him backwards onto the porch. He fell and looked up at me.

"What's wrong?" he asked.

"I said stop!" I yelled at him.

"I'm so sorry. I got carried away," he apologized.

"Go on and get the fuck out of here!" I screamed.

"But I'm not finished," he replied.

"Either you get out of here, or I will kill you," I spoke fiercely.

Cowboy jumped up, pulled up his clothes and ran to his truck. I looked at the weak fool. He almost made me kill his stupid ass over some dumb shit. What the hell was going through his mind?

I walked back into the house with my hand holding my ass. Damn that shit hurt. As I lay in my bed, I began rubbing my ass and playing with my pussy. The thought of him ramming dick in my ass actually excited me. My pussy began to get so moist. I started pushing my index finger in and out, then realized that I didn't hear Cowboy's truck start up. Suddenly, I heard my front door open. I grabbed my 9 mm from under the bed, and waited for him to enter the bedroom. I hadn't locked the front door; never had a reason to, but now this fool was stalking me.

"Ms. Nikki," Cowboy called out.

"Get out of here Cowboy, and go home," I said.

I could hear him walking down my hallway. I pointed the 9 mm at the door waiting on him to enter my bedroom. He was going to die tonight. This wasn't supposed to go down. I'd just moved here, and now I'd have to move again. Damn.

"Ms. Nikki," Cowboy spoke as he stuck his head in and peeped around the door.

"What?" I asked.

"Please forgive me," he said.

"Damn, come on around the corner," I said. I continued, "Why are you in my house? I forgive you, now you can go home."

As I watched him, he moved slowly to my bed. He sat on the bed and began rubbing my thigh. I didn't stop him; I just looked at him like he was crazy. Cowboy pulled off his shoes and got on the

bed. I opened my legs so he could see my pussy. He dived down between my legs, and started licking and sucking my clit.

"Pull off your pants. I want to see what you working with. I want to see it stand to attention," I told him.

He jumped off the bed and pulled down his pants fast. Damn, he was working with something. He looked to be about nine inches. It was thick and long. Just how I liked it.

I motioned for him to lay on the bed so I could do the sixty-nine with him. He lay out like a fat cat. I sat down on his face, and he attacked my pussy like he was hungry. It was kind of hard for me to get to his cock, because he was kind of a big boy. I rubbed his cock as he tongue fucked me.

Getting down lower to suck his cock, he moaned out like a fucking girl. I sucked and sucked him until he busted. I was about to get up, but he pulled me back down on his face, licking me more and more.

About fifteen minutes passed by, and he was still going. I got up and lay on the bed. Cowboy jumped down below and continued to eat me. He licked and licked me until around six o'clock in the morning. I guess we fell asleep; when I woke up his head was still at my pussy but he was asleep. I looked at the clock, and it read nine o'clock. I tried to move out of the way, but he jumped up and pushed his head in my pussy again. Damn, this fool hadn't gotten enough.

After that night I couldn't get rid of Cowboy. For two weeks he came by and licked my pussy every single night. Some nights I

let him fuck. I told him about Jeremy, but he seemed like he didn't give a care.

It was about time to go and bring Jeremy home, and Cowboy was going to help me do it. I had that boy's nose wide open. He would probably kill for me.

I got on the phone, and booked a room at the Rivera Hotel and Casino. Cowboy had a brand new black Dodge Challenger that he said I could use. I was going to Vegas to claim my prize. This time, I would bring Jeremy home. Do-or-Die. Which ever he decided.

Chapter 18

I headed to Vegas, after I packed two suitcases of clothes and all my guns with ammo. Cowboy wanted to go, but there was no way I was taking a witness, or then I would have to kill him off. As I drove away, Cowboy stood in my yard looking like a farmhouse boy. He was my fill-in until Jeremy joined me here in Iuka.

I drove and drove for hours; I had to pull over at a hotel in Wichita, Kansas to rest. I pulled out my HTC cell phone and called Jeremy with my number blocked. To my surprise, he picked up the phone and said hello. I closed my eyes and envisioned us together. After I didn't answer him, he hung up. I laid back on the bed and stared at the ceiling, thinking of how we were going to be together. I couldn't go to Vegas without a plan. Suppose he had another female in his life? Or what if his mother or that punk ass Derek got in my way? I guess they would have to die too. I wouldn't leave without my man.

After a good nights rest in Wichita, I proceeded on to Vegas. As soon as I hit the Nevada state line, I began to fiend for Jeremy. All I could smell was his cum in the air. My thoughts were of his smell, his sex, and the taste of his cum.

I checked into the hotel, took my luggage up, and headed out to Jeremy's house. I turned my tracking device on; he was still

there. I couldn't believe that the device still worked. It'd been weeks since I'd actually checked on him.

First, I drove by Derek's house to see if he was home. His green Buick Century was parked in the driveway with another car. That let me know he would be busy for hours. He always had different bitches at his house. Moving on...

I arrived at Jeremy's house. The lights were on, but no car. It must have been in the garage. I parked across the street from his house looking for any type of movement. It seemed like I sat there for hours when suddenly, the living room light came on. My eyes got big and my heart began to beat heavily.

The light went back off. A few cars rode by, making it kind of hard for me to sneak out and creep up to the house. Finally, the streets were clear. I hopped out of the car, and ran up towards the balcony, jumping behind bush after bush on the way. Finally, I approached the door when I heard noises. It sounded like a female voice coming from the back of the house.

I walked slowly towards the back, and I saw Jeremy and a young bright skinned female sitting in the pool making out. They had the radio blasting. *Click. Click. Click* went my head. My mutha-fucking blood started boiling.

I turned around to walk back to the car to get the 9 mm, but stopped. I turned back around and watched some more. It hurt me so bad to see the love of my life about to fuck that bitch. He acted as if he had forgotten all about me. His kisses seemed more intense than with any other female. Well, I was going to remind him that I still existed.

121

After they finished making out, he got out of the pool and entered the house. This was my chance to go to the pool and confront this bitch. After I made sure he was gone, I walked out into the open. She looked around and jumped.

"What the fuck? Who are you?" she asked.

"Bitch, what are you doing with my man?" I asked politely.

"Bitch? Who the fuck is you?" she asked again.

I looked at her and walked over closer, as I said, "I'm the bitch that's going to take your life." I picked up the radio and threw it in the water. That bitch started jerking and bucking.

"Die bitch die," I said as I looked around for Jeremy. The lights began blinking off and on as she fried in the pool. You could hear the electric shocks very loudly, and fire was popping off the water. I looked at her for a few more seconds, and ran off to my car. If he didn't know by now, he would. NIKKI'S BACK.

Chapter 19

When I pulled up at the hotel, I saw Vegas police cars everywhere. My heart began to beat faster. Damn, have they caught up with me? Instead of driving by, I pulled in to see what was really going on. I didn't want to look too suspicious. The valet person walked up to my car and I asked, "Why are the police here?"

"There was a disturbance in the lobby of the hotel. Everything is under control," he replied. "Okay. Were they arrested?" I asked.

"Yes ma'am," he said.

"Okay, because I thought they were here for me," I said with a fake smile.

"Are you a bad girl?" he joked.

"I'm bad all the time," I replied.

"Yes ma'am," he smiled as he jumped in my car and pulled away to the garage.

I walked up to my room and sat down on the floor next to the hotel window. I looked at the police lights shining so brightly. I was thinking I should get the AK 47 out the trunk and *set it off* in this mutha-fucker. I could kill all those police and everybody that got in my way. My mind was going crazy. I was so fucking mad. I wanted Jeremy so bad that I could taste him. It was killing me to

know that he didn't desire to be with me. You could give a person the world and they still wouldn't appreciate it. I just didn't understand people, but I guess that's life.

I lay back on the floor and looked up at the ceiling. People might believe me to be crazy, but who gives a fuck what they think? There were so many evil thoughts going through my mind that night. Was it possible to get some explosives? A few explosives in my hands would be very dangerous. I could blow up Jeremy's house, Derek's house, and definitely Jeremy's mama's house. That bitch hates me. She's lucky I haven't killed her ass already. I could see myself hitting that bitch in the head, knocking her out. Then I'd put an explosive in her mouth and watch her head blow off her fucking body. It steamed me so bad when I saw that lady. She was always talking against me to Jeremy. And that pussy ass Derek, I never liked him. He never had anything good to say about anybody. He always talked negative.

He's another bitch I would take out before I left Vegas. I could hear all that shit he was telling Jeremy about me. How could he say that I was crazy? I'm not crazy just heart broken. All this pain I'm feeling; who's going to mend my heart? There is so much anger and hurt, that I don't want help. Help for what? I know who I want and what I want. All those bitches standing in my way will be taken out the game. And you better believe that shit.

My mind started racing. Devilish thoughts were embedded in me to go see Derek while it was fresh on my mind. It was Saturday night and I knew he'd be at Club Dreamz tonight. I walked to the bathroom, turned on the shower, and laid out a Becca short black see-through dress. Fuck it; I was going to the club to claim another gift. Derek...

Chapter 20

As I walked through the hotel lobby, I turned so many heads. I was looking oh so fly with my Becca black dress on, that barely covered my ass. The valet pulled up with my car.

"I see you are a bad girl," the young valet I'd talked to earlier said.

"Always," I replied

"Well, I want to see just how bad you are, Ms. Lady," he said.

"I would love that. I'm Nikki," I introduced myself.

"I'm Doug," he stated as he reached in his pocket and handed me a business card.

"Cool," I said.

I got into the car and sat there for a few minutes. I messed with the radio, trying to find my Lil Boosie CD. I put in the CD, and found my song *"Set It Off."* I pulled off and popped me a pill. I'd be jigging tonight for sure.

I pulled up at Club Dreamz, and it was packed. I parked and got out. The line was so far back that many wouldn't get in. I took out my cell and called Leroy. He was the owner of Club Dreamz,

and a nigga I used to fuck a long time ago when I first arrived in Vegas.

"Hello," he answered.

"What's up Leroy?" I asked.

"You must be outside the club," he said.

"Hell yeah, I need to get in. I don't want to stand out here with all these fucking flunkies," I replied.

"Which door are you at?" he asked.

"I'm at your back door. I walked around the club," I replied.

"Bitch, you crazy," he said.

"Why do I have to be all that?" I asked.

"Because you are; but I'm on my way around to meet you," he said as he hung up the phone in my face.

"Damn, he could have given me time to say bye," I spoke out loud to myself.

Leroy hung up and eventually came out to get me. It seemed like he took forever just to get his fat ass to the door. I was standing and looking around, waiting on him. Five minutes went by, and now I'd gotten really angry. "What the fuck is he doing?" I asked myself. Suddenly, the back door opened.

"Damn, Nigga. It took you long enough," I said.

Leroy blocked the door and replied, "Bitch I don't want no trouble tonight. So get in this mutha-fucker and chill."

"Me? Act a fool?" I asked.

"Yeah you. Remember, I used to fuck you. I know you," he replied.

"You make it sound like I'm violent or something," I said.

"Shit, you are. You crazy than a mutha-fucker, but I love that good ass pussy you have. And your head is off the chain. You need to put that shit on the market," he said while laughing.

"I see you are full of jokes tonight," I said sarcastically.

I stepped in his face and placed a kiss on his jaw. As I walked past, he slapped me on the ass gently. I just kept walking.

"I'm serious. Chill," he spoke as he pointed his index finger at me.

"I'll think about it," I replied as I walked off.

I walked through the VIP section, and bitches and niggas were jumping all over the club. They were playing *Becky* by Plies. I eased around the club looking around. Niggas were all over me trying to get some play. I started hearing *Click. Click. Click* in my head.

I shook my head, trying to stop myself. Suddenly, someone put their hands on my shoulders and asked, "Are you alright?"

I turned around to look into the face of Derek. "Yeah Nigga, I'm good," I replied.

"I don't know; you look like you up to some crazy shit," he replied.

"I guess you really believe I'm crazy. You're a damn fool," I said.

"No boo; I just know what Jeremy told me," he said.

"Jeremy could have told you that I was a sniper, and you would've believed it," I said.

"Yeah I would. My nigga has no reason to lie to me. He thinks you off your mutha-fuckin' rocker," Derek said.

"Jeremy doesn't know shit about me. I guess he likes fucking crazy ass women with good pussy," I shot back.

"Shit, if it's that good, give me some. Jeremy once said he didn't care if I hit it," he boasted.

"Well, tell Jeremy to go fuck himself," I said and walked off.

As I walked off, Derek touched me on the ass and said, "Damn girl, you got back." I walked back to him, and got in his face. I planted a small kiss on his jaw and said, "Let's fuck tonight." Then I walked off. Derek had this big ass smile on his face. If I knew him correctly; he would fuck. Dogs will be dogs. I just hoped I didn't come back with fleas.

It was twelve o'clock and I was getting tired. I danced around with Derek and a couple of more niggas. Shit; my feet started to hurt. As I got ready to walk out the door, Derek pulled me by my arm. "Where you going?" he asked.

"To my hotel. My feet are hurting like a mutha. I don't have all night to be waiting on you," I replied.

"Well, I'm headed to the crib; you want to follow me?" he asked.

"Follow you? Nigga I know where you stay," I said.

"How do you know where the fuck I stay?" he rudely asked.

"Calm down, Nigga. Remember Jeremy and I dropped by one evening for drinks?" I asked.

"Yeah, yeah. Damn I forgot about that shit," he said.

"Good, now you don't have to say I'm stalking you," I replied.

"It's all good, Shawty. I'll meet you at the crib," he said.

He walked back inside while I proceeded to my car. Before I could get inside my car, Leroy grabbed my door. "I guess you thought you were leaving without fucking me," he said.

"I'm not fucking you nigga," I said.

"You fucking tonight. I didn't let you in for free," he said while rubbing his cock.

"Not tonight Leroy. How about tomorrow?" I suggested.

"No, bitch. Now. I can pull this mutha-fucker out now and let you suck it, or whip it out and shove it down your throat," he said.

All kind of thoughts began running through my mind again. "Hello!" he yelled.

"What? I can't hear you," I said.

"Here, suck this mutha-fucker," he said while pulling out his little ass dick.

I began sucking his dick like he told me. This nigga had a bad smell to him. That was one of the reasons why we split up; his funky ass didn't want to wash his nuts. I pulled on his cock about three times and began to gag. "Bitch stop playing," he said while grabbing the back of my head.

"Let me go," I said.

"Suck me and don't bullshit me like you did the last time," he spoke while trying to shove it down my throat. I reached under the seat and slowly slid out my switch blade. As I tried to suck Leroy, he slapped me in the back of the head and stated, "Bitch, you can't suck a dick like that. Get into it and stop fucking around. I want to bust a nut."

Before he could finish criticizing me, I stuck my switch blade deep into his nuts and began turning it. Leroy fell to the ground as a little blood spurted up on my dress and face. I stepped out of the car, and kicked him over and over as he yelled out like a little bitch. I looked around to make sure nobody was looking. You could only hear music ringing out into the streets.

"You fucking bitch!" he yelled out.

"Bitch? That's not nice to talk to a lady like that. I warned you about trying to force your dick down my throat. Remember, we had this talk before," I said.

"You bitch. I'm going to kill you," he threatened as he tried to get his walkie-talkie to call in.

I kicked the walkie-talkie away and said, "Bitch, I'm taking your life tonight."

I swung the switch blade back, and cut that bitch right across the mouth. His mouth fell open as I jumped down on him and stabbed him in his eye. I pulled it out and stabbed him in the other eye.

"Die bitch die. You need to wash under your stanking ass nuts," I spoke in a low tone.

It was hard for me to stop; I began stabbing him all in his face and neck. Suddenly I heard someone. I stood up off Leroy and began looking around. He was stupid to try me, because I wasn't scared of getting caught. I looked around, and saw Derek getting in the car. There was a chick getting in on the passenger side of his car, but she didn't look familiar. I looked down at Leroy and he wasn't moving. I wiped my switch blade off on his shirt and got in my car. He wasn't my target for tonight, but an added bonus. Damn, it felt so good to be so bad...

Chapter 21

As I pulled into Derek's driveway, I saw he'd arrived before me. I got out and went in the trunk of my car. There were a few towels in the back, so I tried to clean myself up by wiping off and changing clothes. I walked to the front door; it was halfway open. I just pushed the door open and walked on in. Derek was kneeling down on the floor in front of the door eating that bitch's pussy.

"Hello. I'm here," I called out.

He looked at me, and continued to eat her pussy. I walked over to the couch and looked at them until he said something.

"Girl, pour us some drinks while you drooling," he said.

"Drooling? Looks like you're drooling in her pussy," I said.

"I'm gonna do yours next," he said.

"Bitch please," I replied while heading to the kitchen to fix drinks. This was my chance to drug this nigga. He was making it easy for me to kill his pussy ass. As I fixed vodka and orange juice I poured a little Rohypnol into their drinks. Rohypnol is a date rape drug that I learned about years ago with Marvin. He used some on me the first time we met. Fucking pussy; he shouldn't have taught me everything he knew. That's why he's dead now. Trying to fuck me in the game and got fucked up his damn self.

Derek and his female friend drank those drinks so fast. He gulped his down and continued to eat pussy. A few minutes later, they began fucking like dogs.

Fifteen minutes went by, and Derek said, "Damn, I'm hot. I need to hit the shower."

Before he could leave the living room, his female friend was out cold. I stood up and watched Derek stumble down the hall. He entered the bedroom, and a few seconds later I heard him lay on the bed.

This was perfect. I went to the kitchen and began washing out the glasses.

Click. Click. Click. This shit was popping in my head. I threw the washed glasses down on the floor, breaking them. I looked through the kitchen, and found a huge meat cleaver. It was perfect for my kill. I walked over to the couch; this female was still as if she was already dead. I took the knife and rubbed it against her body, but she still didn't move. I took the meat cleaver and began poking around by her navel; my first thought was to cut her fucking pussy open and watch her bleed slowly. Suddenly, I heard noises coming from the bedroom.

I walked into the room, and I looked at Derek standing up trying to take off his shirt. It was unbelievable that he was still standing. That roofie was taking longer on his black ass.

He took off his shirt and laid out on the bed, flat on his back. There was a chair in the room so I took a seat. I stared at the meat cleaver, wondering how I should kill this pussy ass nigga. He had talked against me to Jeremy since day one. He'd talked all that

noise because he wanted to fuck me. I would have given him some pussy, but for a price.

I thought maybe I should cut off his dick and mail it to his mother. Or maybe I should cut open his chest, pull his heart out, and mail it to the police. It would be fun to hack his body into pieces, and watch him suffer. Or perhaps I should scalp him like the Indians did back in the day. My mind was wondering all sorts of things.

Then it hit me; Derek had a Samurai sword on his front wall. I jumped up, and ran down the hall to see if it was still there. There she was, so shiny and pretty. As I pulled up a chair to the wall to get the sword down, this female starting moaning. I jumped down and ran over to her. "Damn bitch, I thought you would give me a little more time," I said.

I pulled out the sword, and I looked at it with lust in my eyes. It looked so sweet that I got a little excited down below. As I continued to look at the sword, I began to poke her with it. "Bitch, get up," I said.

She moaned, but didn't move; so I pulled her mutha-fucking hair to get her up. She fell down on the floor, looking groggy. "What you doing?" she asked slowly.

"Bitch, you are the one who chose to be here with that piece of shit. It's not my fault," I said.

"Please, let me go," she said.

"Let you go? Do you think I'm about to hurt you? I'm here to save a whore," I joked.

She didn't answer, just leaned over on the end of the couch. "Wake up bitch," I spoke as I kicked her in the stomach.

"Oh please. Don't do this," she slurred while slobbing out the mouth.

"Bitch you are so pathetic," I said.

She called out, "Lord please help me."

"You call on the Lord, but He's not here. I don't see him and I definitely don't hear him," I mocked.

"Just let me live, I won't say a word," she begged.

"Bitch, if you ask me one more time to let you live, I will kill your nasty ass. Stop fucking around and get up," I said.

"I can't move. I can't get up," she sobbed.

She began to sob and cry like a fucking bitch. It really pissed me off because she was weak, just like Nicole. I was always taught to be on my P's and Q's. Never let your guard down. I was still fucking off with this bitch, when I heard Derek again. I headed down the hall when the girl called out again, "Lord, please help me. Just let me go," she said while trying to stand to her feet.

I walked back to her and said, "You calling on the Lord to save you, but I'm the only one here to save you; and right now I'm not in the saving business," as I took the sword and sliced her fucking head off. Blood began spurting up out of her neck as her head rolled under the coffee table. "Sweet," I said out loud while cheesing from ear to ear. Her body hit the floor. Images began to fill my head. I remembered the day my mother beat me for not

finishing my food. I had to stand at the table eating my food, as her and Vanessa sat.

"Mama, I'm not hungry anymore," I spoke.

"You're going to eat every drop of food on your plate," she replied.

"I can't, my stomach hurts," I said.

She jumped up from the table to go get my father's old belt. She came back and began beating me across the back yelling, "Eat that damn food. I work too hard." All you could hear was the belt slapping against my skin as I tried to eat my food. If I fell to the floor, I had to stay there while she beat me like a dog. I couldn't do nothing but yell out and eat my food. That day, after she finished, I had whelps all over my back and on the backside of my arms. I shook my head wishing that image would go away. My mind snapped back to reality.

I looked down at this female and all I could see was my mama's face attached to her body. Swinging the sword back, I began hitting her body over and over, slicing it to pieces. All I could hear was my mama saying, 'I hate you'. I snapped back to reality again, and I heard Derek moan. I walked off like nothing had happened and headed to go finish off Derek.

I entered the bedroom; he had turned over on his right side and knocked the lamp off the table. I stood over the bed waiting for him to move; he did nothing. So, I put the sword down on the bed and sat back in the chair with the meat cleaver in my hand. Should I wake him up now, or wait until he rises on his own? Fuck it, I'm going to wake that pussy up now.

I walked over to the bed, and began poking him with the meat cleaver. I poked with the sharp edge, as a way to let him know I was waiting for him to wake his punk ass up. He began to wake up slowly.

"Bitch, what did you do to me?" he slurred.

"Me? I didn't do anything," I said.

"You fucking bitch. I'm gonna kill you," he muttered.

"Now Derek, those are very harsh words. Kill me? Doesn't look like you can do much of anything right now," I replied.

He tried to get up but I shoved him back down on the bed. "It's funny because you invited me over to your house, when you said I was crazy. You wanted to fuck me. Told Jeremy lies about me, and—" I said.

"Nicole, I'm gonna fuck you up. What the fuck you do to me?" he interrupted.

"Well, I put a roofie in your drink so I could kill you later on. I didn't know you were going to bring someone else home with you. So I had to get rid of her too," I smiled.

"You crazy bitch. Where is she?" he asked.

"Her head is under your coffee table and her body is sliced to pieces on your living room floor. How are you going to explain that?" I asked.

"Bitch, I'm not taking the fall for you," he said.

"I know you're not, because you're going to be dead too. I'm taking your life tonight," I said.

"Nicole don't fucking do this," he pleaded.

My head began to sway from side to side. "What did you call me?" I asked.

"Nicole. You fucking bit—"

Before he could get the word bitch out of his mouth I hacked him across the mouth. His chin lay open while blood oozed out. More blood splashed in my face. His eyes found my face, piercing mine, and I picked the meat cleaver up from his mouth and cut right into his fucking forehead. His skull cracked open like a watermelon. I picked up the meat cleaver and hit that bitch harder in his forehead, until his brain was showing, and blood oozed out of it. I began to laugh at that pussy. I picked up my cleaver, and walked around to the bottom of the bed looking at him laying open, bleeding and shit. When I looked at his dick and noticed that it was rock hard, the responsible woman in me couldn't just let some thick good dick go to waste. I dropped my pants and laid between his legs. I licked his dick from top to bottom to see if it would really stay hard, and when it did, I was amped! I squatted on top of him at an angle and bounced like my life depended on it. At the angle I was in, I was forcing the tip to hit my G-spot vigorously, and I came quick and hard. I even broke into a lil sweat. After I caught my breath, I got down to put my pants back on and then proceeded to get the shit over with.

I got up on the bed, and placed myself between his legs, for my finale. I reached back and hit that nigga in the stomach with

my meat cleaver, and cut him open. I reached inside and pulled out his guts. He smelled like pure death. I pulled and pulled until I was off the bed standing on the floor with guts in my left hand. I threw it on the floor, and looked at Derek.

"You stupid bitch; that was for talking against me to Jeremy. Your mouth is open, but I can't hear you. Why you not talking shit now? Oh my bad, your mouth isn't working. Oh shit, your brain isn't working either," I stated while laughing out loud.

Holding my meat cleaver in the air, I licked the tip of it, tasting blood. While staring at it I said, "How sweet death tastes." Then I perfectly angled the tip of the meat cleaver at the hole of his dick and rammed it through. As I looked at it just hanging in the air from the inside of his dick, I patted my hands together and walked out knowing that justice had been served!

Chapter 22

After taking a shower at Derek's house, I left. I had to wear some of his clothes. As I got into my car, thoughts rushed at me. I had to get Jeremy tonight and leave this fucking city. I'd had too many kills in one night and I'd been so sloppy. Evidence was all over the place. What the fuck was I thinking? My fingerprints were all over the place, and weapons were left everywhere.

"Yes Nikki, the tables have turned," a soft voice called out.

"No. No. No. Not you again," I said.

"You can't keep killing these people like this," the voice said.

"Bitch, I don't have time to clean up. I'm on a mission. Plus, they won't be able to find me once I hit the Nevada state line," I said.

"You will get caught," the voice continued.

"You mean we will get caught. All of this is because of you. I'm protecting you Nicole. I wouldn't do this for nobody else," I replied.

"Nikki, you stop this," Nicole said.

"Nicole, go away bitch. You need to stop trying to run shit. You will never come back. I won't let you," I said.

I drove down the interstate and headed to Jeremy's house. It was time for me to claim my prize. I looked into the mirror and saw this little girl sitting in a swing crying. I jammed on the brakes, turned around and saw nothing but highway. I put my foot back on the gas, and drove on. I rode slowly by the house, and it looked very dark. No lights, no life, no nothing. I continued on, turned my car around, and parked.

I got out of my car and walked to the edge of the driveway. I was staring at his house, when suddenly I heard a car door open. I turned around to see this tall middle-aged white man with a lit cigarette in his mouth walking up to me. "Ma'am can I help you?" he asked.

"No sir, not really. I heard about a death here the other night and came by to be nosey," I lied.

"And who are you?" he asked.

"I'm sorry sir. I'm Nikki." I replied.

"Nikki what?" he pressed.

"Nikki Webb," I told him. Damn that was a stupid move. I'd told him my real name.

"Did you know the young lady?" he asked.

"No sir, but I know the young man that lives here. Jeremy," I replied.

"How do you know him?" he inquired.

"Well, I don't think you need to know all that. Why are you asking me all these questions?" I asked him.

He flipped out his badge and stated, "I'm Agent Paul Pickett."

"Agent? You must be FBI or CIA," I said.

"FBI," he replied.

"Oh wow. Is Jeremy in trouble?" I asked being nosey.

"Why? Do you think he's in trouble?" he answered with a question.

"No sir. I'm sorry for asking questions," I said.

I began to walk off and he said, "Here take my card. If you hear anything, please let us know."

"Okay sir," I said as I took his card.

Agent Pickett watched me as I got into my car and pulled off. It looked as if he was taking down my license plate number. Damn, I know I must move tonight.

I took Jeremy's tracking device out of my glove compartment and turned it on. Beeping noises were ringing out. My device was about dead. Damn.

I hurried and looked at the device to try to find out where he was. Damn. To my surprise, he was at his mother's house. It might be hard for me to get to him. I just hoped I didn't have to fuck her up to get to her son.

DeRanged

I rode past Jeremy's mama's house, and saw his car pulled in the driveway crooked. I pulled down the street to park between two of the neighbors houses, got out and walked back up towards the house. I stood in the front yard on the grass, and just stared up at the house. It was kind of big, and I wondered how I could grab this fool up out of here without waking up his mother or his brother.

It was five o'clock in the morning. I ran up toward the house and began searching around for an unlocked window, but was very careful not to wake anyone. It seemed like every room had a television on, which made it possible for me to look in clearly. I could see Jeremy's mama laid out snoring loud as hell. Her legs were gapped open and she lay in the middle of the bed. His little brother was on the couch in the living room. Every window in the house was locked except for the bathroom window. The light in there shined very brightly.

I slowly raised the bathroom window, after I found a bucket to stand on, and climbed in. As I stepped in, the 9 mm fell out of my back, hitting the floor. I squatted down, hoping it didn't wake anyone. Especially his stupid ass mama. After a few minutes of not hearing any movement, I proceeded on through the house. I stepped out of the bathroom, and crept from room to room looking; there was no Jeremy. I stepped up to his mama's room, and pulled out the magazine to my weapon. I opened the door slowly, stepped in, and walked up to the bed. She lay there sleeping peacefully. It bothered me so bad that she had tried to keep me and Jeremy apart. I poked her with the 9 mm to wake her up. She began to rub her eyes and opened them. As soon as she saw me, her mouth fell open. Before she could say a word, I

cracked that mutha-fucker in her head with the butt end of the gun. Right between her eyes; I hit her so hard that it split the skin open. Her head fell backwards on the pillow as blood oozed downwards.

I looked around the room to find a weapon, and saw two solid wood lamps with gold paint. I walked over and picked one up; the lamp was very heavy, but not heavy enough for me to crack this lady's skull. I stood over her as she lay back on the bed. I lifted the lamp and banged and banged and banged her head into the pillow. Blood covered the walls, the bed, the floor, and even me. I hadn't planned to kill her, but once I saw her ugly ass face and thought about all the bad stuff she had said about me, I had to kill her.

Finally, I stopped and tossed the lamp next to her. It looked like she was still moving. I saw a leather belt hanging off her mirror next to the closet. I walked over and got the belt, and began popping the belt together, making a clapping sound. My eyes must have been playing tricks on me; I thought I saw her move. I stood there waiting for her to move again. I began beating her with that leather belt. She needed an ass beating for all the shit that had come out of her mouth. I hate a messy ass female. She wanted Jeremy to have the female she liked. I didn't give a fuck if the bitch liked me or not. After giving her a couple of hits with the belt; I tossed it. It wasn't doing what I wanted done. My mind started wondering what I should do. I remembered a shed was in the back with an axe at the door. I eased out the bedroom and into the kitchen to the back door. I walked up to the shed; the axe lay in plain view. I picked up the axe and swung it once. This

was what I was looking for. As I walked back towards the house, I began to have flashbacks.

My mind started wandering back to my mama. Vanessa, Mama, and I were sitting in the living room watching television. We were watching *The Hills Have Eyes.* A scary part came on, and Vanessa jumped on the couch with Mama, and Mama hugged her. My mind was telling me to do it too, but my body wouldn't move. I was looking from the television to Mama, wondering what I should do. Finally, my body let me go and I ran over and jumped on the couch with them. I grabbed her left arm because Vanessa was on the right side. She moved Vanessa out of the way and got up. She reached and grabbed me by my pig tails, and pulled me up off the couch. Mama pulled me back over to the other couch and said, "You sit here."

Then she sat back next to Vanessa and they hugged up again. At that moment, I knew I was an outcast. It never occurred to me to figure out the reason why she treated me so bad. I just accepted it as being Mama's ways. My heart fell down in my panties and I began to sweat. I began fiddling with my fingers and looked at the two of them on the couch. They seemed to be so happy. It hurt me so, because this was my flesh and blood treating me like I was nothing to her. As I walked back inside the house to the bedroom, I snapped back to reality, and I saw Jeremy's mother laying there with no face. I'd beaten her face to a pulp. I stood there and gritted my teeth together.

"That's for not wanting me to love Jeremy," I spoke as I turned around and looked at myself in the mirror. I lifted the axe and began chopping away. As I chopped her up, the memory of her

being in the hospital talking shit rushed into my mind; I also thought about a barbecue she'd had at her house where she was talking shit, and a couple of times over at Jeremy's house where she was talking shit. Now her ass lay here fucked up; what the fuck can she say now? I hate messy bitches. After I finished separating her body, I chopped her head straight off her body and tossed the axe to the side.

"Nikki, you have to stop. Your fingerprints are all over that axe," Nicole said.

"I don't give a fuck about that; after I get Jeremy, they will never see me again. I'm going to kidnap his ass and we will be long gone before anyone finds this body," Nikki replied.

"I'm scared you're leaving too much evidence. They're going to catch us," Nicole said.

"Bitch, stop being a pussy like the rest of them. We aren't going to get caught. That's why we have to keep moving," I replied.

"Okay Nikki, but you're leaving too much shit behind," Nicole stated.

"Fuck that. Let's go. I'm not worried about that shit. I'm not leaving without my prize," I replied while picking up the axe and walking out the door.

I moved on down the hall toward the kitchen; his little brother lay quietly on the couch. I stood behind the couch just staring at him. My mind kept clicking to kill him off, but my heart wouldn't let me. Nicole couldn't kill a kid.

"Nicole, we need to kill this kid before he wakes up and sees us," I said.

"Fuck that Nikki; I'm not killing any kids. I've tried to talk to you, but I refuse to let you kill that kid," Nicole said.

"Since you won't do it, I will do it," I boasted.

"No Nikki. Please don't. Let's just go find Jeremy," Nicole said.

"Damn Nicole, you are such a fucking chicken. He would have been an easy kill," Nikki said.

"Let's go Nikki. Now," Nicole demanded.

"Fuck that Nicole. You just close your eyes because I'm going to kill this little mutha-fucker," I said.

I walked around to the front of the couch and looked down at this little boy. He was innocent and pure, but he had to be killed. I didn't want anyone to witness seeing me, even though he was asleep. He might have overheard me killing his mother and pretended to be asleep. I sat down on the big glass table and stared at him for a few minutes. Raising the axe, I looked at it and saw the blood dripping off of it.

"Nikki, you know this is not fair," Nicole spoke.

"Shut the fuck up, Nicole. You are such as wimp. I'm not leaving any witnesses," I retorted.

"I'm just scared. We need to leave," Nicole replied while breathing hard.

Suddenly, the little boy woke up. He looked at me, and I looked into his eyes. He wiped his eyes, asked, "What are you doing here?" and turned over to go back to sleep. I jumped up and began to panic.

"Damn Nikki, he saw us. I told you we need to leave. I don't want you to kill no kids. This kid has done nothing to us." Nicole said.

"Sure he hasn't, but he won't live to tell anything," Nikki stated as she turned around and lifted the axe in the air. The first chop went across his lower back. She chopped and chopped until he was in pieces laid out on the couch. The last thing she separated was his head from his body. Then she chopped the head straight down the middle, slicing it in half. One half of his head fell down towards the floor. Nikki stepped back; the kid was splattered all over the couch. Body parts were everywhere.

"Nikki, what have you done?" Nicole called out to me.

"We can't leave any witnesses. You need to get your fucking self together before I really go off on you. What the hell is going on with you?" Nikki asked.

"Nikki, you just killed a fucking kid. An innocent kid. What the fuck is wrong with you?" Nicole shot back.

"Bitch, you were talking about leaving evidence and fingerprints behind. So why should I leave witnesses behind? What's the fucking difference?" Nikki asked.

"Nikki, you are crazy. You leave evidence, but no witnesses. That kid was innocent. He didn't do anything to you," Nicole explained.

"Bitch, get a grip," I said.

I'd searched the entire house, and no fucking Jeremy. I was really pissed off now. Where in the fuck could that nigga be? Before I left, I looked back at Jeremy's little brother all chopped on the couch.

This wasn't turning out good because I had to get him tonight. The FBI was involved, and there had been too many deaths tonight. I'd been very sloppy and it would all link right back to me. As I closed the front door, I stood out on the grass.

"Damn, where in the fuck is he at?" I asked myself. I continued, "Damn. Damn. Damn."

"Nikki, leave him alone," Nicole said.

"Fuck you. Get out my fucking head," Nikki replied.

"I love Jeremy. You can't hurt him. Please Nikki," Nicole begged.

"Get out my head bitch," I repeated as we stood in the yard looking at Jeremy's car.

I walked over to the car, looked in, and there was Jeremy. A smile came over my face. I was all in his mama's fucking house searching, and this bitch was outside asleep in the car. I stood on the outside of the driver's side looking down at him. He appeared to be passed out drunk. The seat was laid all the way back. This

was my chance. I had to hurry up because the sun was starting to rise.

I opened the driver's door as he rose up, looking all drunk and shit. I took the butt end of my gun and busted him in his face. Blood rushed out of his head as he fell backwards onto the seat. His body lay helplessly. Damn. How in the fuck was I going to get this nigga out the car? Not rushing, I sat down on the door frame pondering to myself. Finally, a solution hit me.

I ran down the street to return to my vehicle. I headed back to the driveway and backed my car up to his door. I struggled and struggled, trying to get him in the truck of my car. My strength was amazing, because I succeeded. I guess it was the adrenaline rushing through my body. After I got him in the trunk, I hog-tied him just like Cowboy taught me to. I tied his hands together, and then tied his feet together, with a rope connecting to both. I took my duct tape, and placed a piece on his mouth. There was this warm feeling coming over me. He lay there just like a baby. So sweet, so innocent. I got in the trunk and lay on top of Jeremy, hugging him. It'd been a very long time since I'd touched him. The feeling was so good that I had an orgasm right then and there.

Suddenly, I heard a car coming down the street. I closed the trunk and jumped in my car. It looked like a Chevy Tahoe. I got down in my seat, and the vehicle slowly crept past Jeremy's mama's house. My heart began to beat faster and faster, as the SUV drove past and the lights disappeared. I cranked up and jetted out like I was on the Indiana Raceway 500. That Tahoe looked like the one Agent Paul Pickett had been driving. I just bet he recognized my car. Damn, I had to leave Vegas now. About the time he found all those dead bodies, I would be long gone from

the crime scenes. Fuck that; I'd come too far to get caught. My heart was pounding so hard.

As I rushed down the street, I looked in the rear view mirror and saw car lights. They were far behind, and then they turned off.

"That's the police following us," Nicole spoke.

Looking back again, I said, "No, they turned off the highway."

"What does that mean?" she asked.

"Bitch, you watch too many cop shows. That vehicle is gone the other way; and what does it matter? We have Jeremy. If the police gets behind us, then we will all die; because I'm not going down without a fight," I said.

"Nikki, I don't want to die," Nicole said.

"I'm not going to let anything happen to you. Stop worrying so much. Stop being such a big ass baby all the time," I said as I sped down the street thinking maybe Nicole was right about the police.

Chapter 23

I drove down the interstate, and I finally had my golden prize. I should go ahead and kill him now, but that would be too easy. I had gone through so much for this sorry ass nigga, and he didn't want me. I looked in the mirror, and I could see a fragile little girl sitting in a charcoal gray swing set looking out into the trees with tears in her eyes. As tears fell down her face, I began to cry. That little girl was feeling pain and hurt. Suddenly, my mind jumped back to reality, as I heard a car horn blowing and honking. I turned my attention back to the street and saw an eighteen-wheeler headed straight for me. I jerked the car to the right side of the road as my tires went spinning. I ran off to the side of the street, landing on the dirt part of it, and I jammed on brakes. My heart was racing and beating 100 miles per hour.

"Damn, Nikki you could have killed yourself," I spoke out loud.

"You mean us," Nicole voiced.

"Get out of my head Nicole. I told you to leave me alone, before I do something bad," I said.

"Nikki, all this killing has got to stop. Why are you doing this?" Nicole replied.

"Because bitch, they hurt us and I'm going to hurt them. I'm going to keep killing until we don't feel anymore pain," I replied angrily.

"Let Jeremy go Nikki," Nicole pleaded.

"Fuck Jeremy. You are lucky I haven't killed him yet; and I will kill him," I said.

"I won't let you," Nicole said.

"Bitch, how are you going to stop me?" I yelled as I popped the trunk and got out of the car with my 9 mm in my hand. It was cocked and ready to rock.

As I popped the trunk, and looked down at Jeremy, I saw he was bleeding from the forehead. His eyes were barely open. When I put the gun to his head, he began to whimper like a fucking baby. This was the first time I'd ever seen him cry. Tears fell down his face like water from a faucet. My heart began to melt like heated butter.

"Don't do this Nikki. Please don't hurt Jeremy. I love him so much," Nicole whimpered.

"Bitch, he's a dog. You can't love dogs. Dogs have to be put down when they are bad," I spat.

"Nikki, please," Nicole asked.

"Bitch, all of this is because of you. We're going to get caught fucking off with Jeremy and all the rest of this bullshit you have gotten us into, because of love. What the fuck does love have to

do with anything? He used you," Nikki said as she pushed the gun into his head.

"Nikki no. Stop!" Nicole yelled.

We both began struggling over the gun. It went off into the air, firing one shot. We fell on the ground fighting each other.

"Nikki, you have to be stopped. I can't let you hurt any more innocent people," Nicole said.

"Try and stop me. All this is for you Nicole. Why are you fighting me?" Nikki yelled out.

"You can't hurt Jeremy. I won't let you hurt him like you did the others," Nicole replied.

"Okay, stop this bullshit," Nikki said.

We lay on the ground looking up at the sky. An image of the little girl on the swing appeared again. She was crying, when all of a sudden, a loud voice rang from the house. It was the voice of her mother yelling and screaming. The middle aged lady came out of the house, walked up to the little girl, and slapped her across the face; knocking her out of the swing. Her body hit the ground as she cried out. The lady grabbed her by the hair and dragged her back towards the house. Nicole began to whimper.

"Bitch, get up and lets go before someone sees us," Nikki said.

"Okay, but don't hurt Jeremy. Please," Nicole begged.

"Let's go bitch. We don't have all day to fuck around with this loser," Nikki said.

We got up and dusted off. I walked back over to the car and looked at Jeremy. I turned his head towards me and put the gun in his mouth. I said to him, "If you do anything, I will kill you. Do you understand?" Jeremy shook his head up and down, saying yes. As I started closing the trunk, I smiled and said, "You weak ass nigga," and slammed the trunk back down.

As I sat in the car, the images of that little girl kept invading my mind. I'd been having dreams and images of her ever since I killed Marvin. He was the one who'd brought me back to life. He was to blame for all of this. If I could kill him again and again and again, I would do so. However, the reality of it was, that little girl was me.

I was shaking my head violently. I wanted this memory to go away. Why did Mama have to hurt me? I was just a little girl, wanting to be loved. She stole my childhood, and I would never forgive her for that.

The image popped up in my head about Mama being on her knees before I killed her. She tried to say that she loved me but she kept stuttering, not wanting to say anything. How could she treat her daughter that way? That's why I killed her mutha-fucking ass, because she wanted to play me for a weak one. Stupid bitch. I hate when bitches lie.

Suddenly Nicole opened the door and began throwing up. She threw up so much that a little blood appeared. Damn, I hoped we were not pregnant, but I had been fucking Jeremy with no condom. I would love to have a child by Jeremy. This would be my chance to keep him with me. He wouldn't dare leave me with a child on the way. Whenever I got a chance; I would get a

pregnancy test. After getting back into the car I thought to myself, *Nicole is so weak*. She closed the car door and laid her head back on the head rest of the car.

"Bitch, you are going to get us busted. Let's go. How many times do I have to tell you? Do you not see cars passing by and people looking at us?" Nikki asked.

"I see those fucking cars Nikki. Don't you see that I'm sick? I'm throwing up, and not feeling well. Damn, stop messing with me all the damn time," I told her.

"Bitch, I'm trying to keep our feet on the ground and not in a fucking jail cell. Are you ready to go to prison?" Nikki asked me.

"No, I'm not going to prison. If we get busted; you're going by yourself," I said.

"Bitch, if I go down. You go down. We will always be together as one and don't you ever forget that!" Nikki scolded.

I turned on the car and headed back down the interstate again. This time I was speeding because we had lost so much time fucking off with Nicole's weak ass. If she kept this up, then I would have to kill her too.

"Nikki, I can hear you," Nicole reminded.

"So bitch, I'm so tired of you trying to stop me. You don't own me," Nikki said.

"You have hurt too many people because you are angry," Nicole said.

"You started this Nicole. You brought me into your life to protect you. Why are you so against me? Haven't I stopped all your hurt and pain?" Nikki asked.

"Yes, you have, but I don't want this anymore," Nicole replied.

"You don't want what; me protecting you?" Nikki asked.

"I want you to protect me Nikki, just stop killing people. We both are hurting," Nicole said.

"Bitch, I'm not hurt. You are the weak one; I can handle me. I'm trying to get you to come on board and stop all this fucking crying," Nikki said.

"If you keep this up, I will have to get rid of you," Nicole spoke softly.

"Bitch, are you serious? I'm here for life and don't you forget that."

"I will find a way to stop you," Nicole said.

"Who are you going to stop? Bitch, you are too weak. I'm stronger than you. You have enjoyed all of this. You love to see someone else hurt just like you," Nikki pointed out.

The conversation ended because it was true. Nicole loved it just as much as I did. As I drove on, I had to stop and get gas. I pulled over at *Shakhty's Convenience Store* and pulled the car up to the gas pump, I saw about three truck drivers just standing around chatting. I hoped Jeremy didn't try anything, because I would pop the trunk and kill him right here, right now.

As I got out, they all began staring at me. I walked up to the store and one guy spoke, "Hello Ms. Lady."

"Hello gentlemen."

The guy that spoke looked like he was about five foot six and in his early forties. He had a salt and pepper mustache and beard. His face was kind of fat and round, and he was a little chubby for his height.

I walked on past them and paid for my gas. I bought chips, candy, and a Pepsi for snacks. I paid thirty dollars for my gas, and proceeded to the pump.

"Can I help you pump that gas, Ms. Lady?" one of the gentleman asked.

"Yes sir, you sure can. I don't want the gas smell all over my new dress."

"Yes, it is a pertty dress," he said.

"Thank you. Do you live around these parts?"

"Yeah ma'am, I do live around hurr. Bout a quowter of a mile yonder way," he replied.

"It sure is quiet around here," I said.

"Yeah ma'am. It sure it," he stated as he finished pumping the gas.

After the gentleman finished pumping the gas I said, "Thank you   sir."
"Anytime ma'am."

After he pumped the gas, I sat down in the vehicle. My mind began wandering again. I looked down at the empty needle I had on the seat. I remember reading that an air bubble in the blood stream will *kill you*. I looked up at the truck driver and smiled. I had on a short pink dress with pink thongs. I took off my thongs and opened the car door.

"No Nikki, don't do this. Just leave now. He has done nothing to you," Nicole pleaded.

"Fuck you Nicole, this one is on me," I said as I exited the car.

Walking back up to the store I asked, "Is there a rest room here?"

"Yes, Ms. Lady. There sure is. It's around the co'nna," spoke the man with the salt and pepper mustache.

"Thank you sir," I replied seductively.

I walked around the corner then looked back at him to follow me. I motioned for him to come on. As I was about to enter the rest room, I saw him coming around the corner.

"Nikki, don't do this," Nicole invaded.

"Not now Nicole. Not now."

"There are people in front of the store. You are going to get us caught," Nicole said.

"I have skills Nicole. We won't get caught. I promise," I said.

The guy entered the rest room closely behind. "Do you want to fuck me?" I asked.

"Hell yeah. You look so pertty," he said.

"I taste delicious too," I added.

"Let me be the judge of that. Can I taste it?" he asked.

"Sure," I replied as I sat on the white sink and lifted my legs into the air. I laid my body back and put my feet on the edge. It exposed my shaved pussy. He walked over rubbing his cock through his pants. He was already hard as a brick. This man began licking my sweet pussy like no tomorrow.

"Damn gal, you sure taste good," he stated as he darted his fat tongue in and out.

"I know; just keep eating my pussy," I spoke as I shoved his head deeper.

His tongue was fat and felt so good. I closed my eyes and pretended it was Jeremy. My mind went back to when Jeremy had bent my legs back and sucked on my clit. He loved running his tongue past my asshole. A few times he would stick his tongue in my ass, making me jump. Then he'd bite me on my ass cheeks. What I liked about Jeremy is that he's a biter. I love to be bitten, especially when I'm about to nut in his face.

My memory faded away when I felt this guy enter my pussy.

"No, I'm not fucking. Pull out," I said.

"I wanna fuck you. I'm not stopping," he said.

He rammed me over and over, as I pleaded for him to stop.

"Stop! No. Stop. Get off me," I pleaded as I began slapping him upside the head.

"Hell no. You teased me with the pussy. I'm fucking," he said as he banged me.

I began pushing him off me and he smacked me right across the face. My body froze up as my head began making those clicking noises again. He hit me so hard, my head hit the mirror behind me and cracked it. My body went limp for a few minutes. After I got myself together, I watched him fuck me some more. I didn't think I could take another lick like that. As this old fool continued to fuck me, I took the needle out of my bra. His eyes were closed tight.

"You shouldn't go around raping women," I stated as I stabbed him with the needle in the neck pushing the air deep within his vein. He grabbed his neck and stumbled backwards but was still standing. I was about to get off the sink when it gave away and fell. My ass hit so hard on the floor that it had me in a daze. My body went limp for another few minutes. I sat there trying to get my thoughts together, and then stood up. After standing for a few seconds, I jumped forward and karate kicked his ass backwards. He fell down and hit his head against the toilet, and it made a loud thump. He rolled over slowly as his eyes stared back at me. He didn't move another inch. I walked over to him, and took the needle out of his neck. I kept stabbing him in the neck with the needle until it broke off. Then I opened his mouth, and pushed the rest of the needle's stem down his throat. "No means no, you dumb fuck," I said.

I looked into the mirror at myself, and straightened up my dress and hair. Then I looked at this man lying dead on the floor. A smile came across my face. A sigh released from my lips. My heart became weak, and I began to cry. I sat down on the floor looking at this dead man and began crying out of control. Thoughts rang out in my head *"Nicole, what are you doing? You can stop her. Her power is strong because of you. You have to end this."*

I rocked back and forward, until I thought about Jeremy. "Oh my god, he's in the car!" I exclaimed as I jumped up off the floor, straightened my dress, and cleaned my face. As I exited the rest room, I saw the other two men standing at the back of my car. "What the fuck?" I called out to them.

The older man of the two stated, "We thought we heard some noises coming from your trunk. What you got in there?" he asked.

"Why? It's nothing but luggage," I replied.

The younger man spoke, "Well, whatever it is, we don't hear it anymore."

"That's because you two old fools are crazy. Why would anything be moving around in my trunk? Are you two listening to my luggage?" I asked.

"You might have a body in there," the younger man joked.

"A body? Now, do I look like the type of girl that would have a body in my trunk?" I asked as I lifted my leg and put my heel on the back of the car, exposing my shaved pussy.

The older man bent down and took a good look. The other one just smiled at me. He had the dirtiest rotten looking teeth I

had ever seen before in my life. He grabbed his dick and rubbed it, trying to get it hard. "Well gentlemen, it seems like I have spent enough time here," I spoke as they drooled over me.

"Sorry about that ma'am. We just thought we heard noises," the older man spoke.

"Where's Earl?" the younger man asked.

"Oh, he's in the rest room cleaning up. He will be out in a few minutes," I replied as I opened my car door to get in.

The two men walked away from the car back up to the store. I sat down, popped the trunk and got out. Opening the trunk, I looked Jeremy in the face eye to eye. I bent over in the trunk and said to him, "If you ever try that shit again, you will die."

He was itching to taste my 9 mm in his mouth. After giving him that evil eye, I closed the trunk. The two men were staring at me.

"It's just my luggage," I said.

"Oh okay," the older man replied.

"You have a safe trip ma'am," the younger man stated as he waved. I waved back.

I sat back down in the car and drove off. These clicking noises were coming more frequently. My head began to start banging. My headaches were becoming more severe. I looked in my purse, and saw a bottle of Excedrin and a bottle of ecstasy.

"Go on and take some ecstasy," Nikki spoke.

"I can't right now. I have Jeremy in the car, and I have to be very careful," I said.

"Bitch, are you serious? We've been getting high together; now today you don't want to? Look at that bottle; doesn't it look good?" Nikki asked as she urged me on. She continued, "Pick it up and smell it."

I picked up the bottle and took the lid off. The scent hit my nose and I couldn't control myself. I stuck the pill in my mouth and swallowed. Nikki said, "That's my girl."

"You're getting out of control Nikki," I said.

"Bitch, I'm so tired of you. You're about to make me do something I don't want to do. If he tries anything again, I will get rid of him. There will be no talking to you," Nikki said.

"Every time I turn around, it seems like you are threatening me about Jeremy. You talk about me; look at yourself," I said.

"Bitch, look at yourself. There is nothing wrong with me. I've been protecting you forever and now you want to bring someone else in the picture," Nikki said.

"Is this about jealousy Nikki?" I asked looking in the rearview mirror.

"Jealousy? I'm not worried about that nigga taking my place. We will always be together as one. You seem to be forgetting that," Nikki stated.

"How can I forget Nikki? You are with me all day everyday. You are my life," I replied.

"You damn right. I am your life," Nikki said.

I pulled out onto the street and started down the highway. Nikki took over again. My mind kept telling me to go back and kill those two old ass men. If I didn't kill them; they would be witnesses and say that they saw me at the store.

"I thought you never left witnesses Nikki. You killed an innocent kid, but left those grown ass perverts," Nicole spoke out.

"Fuck that. I'm going back to kill them and you're going to help me," I replied as I turned the car around in the middle of the highway. I pulled over to the side of the road and popped the trunk. I looked down at Jeremy and realized that I had all my weapons back there with his punk ass. He could have gotten loose and killed me. Damn, I was slipping like a mutha-fucker. I moved Jeremy and reached over behind him. I pulled out all the weapons and placed them on the back seat of the car and covered them up. I picked up the Air Force Talon SS and loaded it up. I placed it on the front seat pointing down towards the floor, and I drove back to the store.

As I pulled back up, the two men stood there looking at me. I pulled close enough to the store to take them out and the clerk inside. I got out, bent over with my ass in the air, and slowly took the Air Force Talon SS out. He was loaded and ready to rock. I slowly lifted the weapon from the car, and pointed it at the store. The two men saw what I had in my hand and tried to run. I began scattering bullets everywhere. I took the two men out first, and then began shooting up the store. I killed up everything that moved. Luckily it was a country ass store out in the middle of nowhere, or else I would've been in a world of shit.

After spraying them fools with bullets and killing them, I jumped into the car and took off. When I put my weapon in the vehicle; it was still smoking. I didn't stop shooting until I emptied the magazine. I headed back down the road again and then Nicole started in on me talking all her bullshit again.

"What the fuck is wrong with you Nikki?" she asked.

"Nicole, stop bugging me about small shit. You know why I'm doing what I do. I have to kill all the witnesses, because I sure as hell don't want to go to jail," I said.

"Well, maybe you do need to go to jail. You are killing innocent people," Nicole taunted.

"Bitch, stop saying these people were innocent. They wanted to hurt you, but I killed them before they got a chance to do anything. I promised that I would protect you and I will. I'm not going to be like Vanessa or your father. They both didn't protect you," I replied.

"My father has nothing to do with this," Nicole said.

"He has a lot to do with protecting you. Where is he now? He's dead, you stupid bitch. How can he protect you?" I asked Nicole.

"Fuck you Nikki. Don't ever talk about my father that way again. He was a good father; he can't help it that he died," Nicole shot back.

"Oh my bad. He couldn't help it that he fucked his daughters either," I mouthed off.

"You are really about to get me upset Nikki. Stop talking about my father, and I'm not playing with you. I just don't understand. Why are you killing people; because you're so angry?" Nicole asked.

"Bitch, I'm not angry. I'm pissed."

Chapter 24

As I drove down the highway, I turned on the radio and Amanda Perez's song, *Good Bye* was playing. I turned up the radio to blasting. The words she sang really touched my heart, and tears started falling down my face. When I first heard that song, I thought she was talking about love, but she was talking about the death of her mother. The song was about how she loved her mother and wanted another chance to see her. It made me think about the special times I'd had with my father. The day of his funeral was so tragic for me. My mother was a cold hearted bitch that day. It made me wonder why God had still allowed me to be in that woman's life. She didn't love me, and definitely didn't want me around. I guess since my father had died, she wanted me gone too.

The day before the funeral, they had the body sitting out for viewing. All his friends, family, co-workers, and ex co-workers came by to show their respects. His coffin was black with gold handles, and the inside was pure white. They had a center piece made out of red roses with white stems. I sat on the front seat in front of his coffin and cried all day. I knew now that he was gone, I would never be treated right. My father had always been my protector. My sister and mama hated me for some reason. Sisters

were supposed to be close, but we were far from close. Everything to her was about a competition, such as, who would win the love of my father. She was upset because he loved me more than her. She knew Mama despised me, so when Father died, it was her opportunity to get back at me. All I ever wanted was to be loved and protected.

People came by giving me hugs. That day was the first time my mama ever sat next to me. I believe she only did it because our relatives stood by. My Aunt Rosetta sat next to me as well. She was my father's baby sister. She knew how Mama treated me; I'd heard her more than a few times get on Mama about it. I wished Aunt Rosetta would have taken me home with her that day; because after that day, my life became a living hell.

It was time for them to close the casket that evening until the next morning, but I didn't want to let go. I stood next to the casket and watched my father.

"God, why did you have to take my father? He's the only somebody who loved me. Please bring him back Lord. I'll give you everything I have. You can have Bonnie and Farrow, but bring Father back home," I said as I cried.

Aunt Rosetta got up and held me. "Baby, your father is in a better place," she said.

"I don't want him there. I want him home with me," I said.

"Well, baby he can't. God has taken your father home with him," she replied.

"Why did God take him away? Why did He take him away from me, Aunt Rosetta?" I asked.

"Baby, this is a part of life. Everyone has to die one day," she tried to explain.

I whispered in a very low tone, "They are going to treat me bad, now that Father's gone,"

"I know baby. I know. I'll do whatever I can to protect you," she stated as she looked over at my mama. She seemed like she wanted to beat her ass that day.

After we left the funeral home, my mama locked me in my room for the rest of the night. She didn't feed me or give me water. I got in my small white wooden twin bed and curled up under the comforter. I stared at the window waiting on the moon to shine in my room. I couldn't turn on the light because I probably would have gotten beaten. After waiting and waiting, I finally went to sleep.

I kept hearing this clicking noise above my head. My eyes were rolling around in my head, and I was scared to open my eyes. The clicking noises got louder and louder. I finally opened my eyes and my mama stood there with a stick in her hand tapping on my bed post. It shocked me so bad, I almost pissed on myself. The moon glared in her face and I could see the evil in her eyes.

"Tomorrow at the funeral, you better not shed a tear. Not one tear. If you so much as cry, I will beat you right there where you stand," she threatened.

"What's wrong Mama? Why?" I asked in a low tone.

"Don't say another word! You know your father didn't love you. He just put up with you because I didn't want to deal with you. You are evil," she replied.

"My father loved me. He told me everyday," I replied.

"Look at you. You back talking me?" she asked.

"No ma'am. Why you hate me so much? Why Mama?" I asked.

She didn't answer; only ran up to the bed and grabbed me around the neck, choking me. I couldn't breath. I pulled on her fingers, trying to get her hands off.

"Mama, no. Stop it," Vanessa called out from the door. She looked very scared.

Mama looked over at Vanessa and released me. She looked down at me and walked out of the room. Before she closed the door, she looked back at me and said, "I'm sorry." She held her head down and closed the door. That was the first and only time I had ever heard my mama say she was sorry. For a minute, I thought she really did have a heart.

The next day at the funeral, we followed the body from the funeral home. My mama didn't want to be in the limousine they provided, so the only person who rode in it was me. At that moment, I felt happy to ride in a limo but then the sadness overwhelmed me again. I always thought family was supposed to be together.

As we walked in the church and sat down, I couldn't help but stare at the huge black casket. It felt strange sitting there. My mama sat between me and Vanessa. She had Vanessa all hugged up, and I was just sitting there with no one. I looked at them two cry as Pastor John Blackwell preached about my father. Tears crawled down my face because I wanted her to hold me too. I looked back at the second row at Aunt Rosetta and she stared back at me.

She whispered, "Do you want me to come up there with you?"

I nodded yes. I didn't want to say anything that would provoke this old woman next to me. During the sermon, Aunt Rosetta came up and slid Mama over like it was nothing. She sat next to me and put her arms around me. It felt good to finally have someone to embrace me. I knew that Aunt Rosetta loved me. I was kind of scared to cry at first because of Mama's threats, but I couldn't help it. As soon as they opened the coffin, I cried out louder and louder. I ran up to the coffin, and I held on to my father. I was screaming and screaming.

It was a very sad day for me. Aunt Rosetta held on to me until it was over. I didn't look up at my mama at all. Even with my eyes closed, I could feel the evil look and hatred.

After the funeral, Aunt Rosetta walked me over to the limousine.

"She's riding with me," Mama said as she jerked me out of Aunt Rosetta's arms.

"You going to hell Janice, for treating that child the way you do," my aunt said.

172

"Fuck you Rosetta. This is my child. I raised her," my mama replied.

"Any animal can raise a child," Aunt Rosetta mocked.

Mama pulled me on toward the car. "I want to stay with Aunt Rosetta," I said.

"Let me have her Janice; since you don't want her. I will take good care of her," my aunt said to Mama.

Everyone was standing outside; I broke away from her and ran to Aunt Rosetta. "Please don't let her take me. She's going to beat me," I yelled out.

"Janice please," Aunt Rosetta begged.

"No. Nicole is my child!" Mama yelled out.

Mama came over to us and snatched me away. I tried to break away again, and she slapped me across the face, knocking me to the ground.

"Janice, how dare you hit that child on church ground? You are evil!" she yelled out as she grabbed my mama's dress pulling her away from the car. My mama turned around and hit Aunt Janice in the chest. They began fighting each other like cats and dogs. These two sisters were throwing blow for blow like Mayweather and Pacino. Uncle James never moved out of the driver seat of the car. He just looked at them two fight. A couple of people from the funeral ran over to break them up. I was on the ground crying and looking up at them fight a few feet from me.

After they separated the two women, Mama said, "You have no right to tell me how to raise my child."

"I do if you're abusing her. Just let her live with me. You don't have to beat her or mistreat her like you're ignorant. She's a child Janice; not some animal," my aunt said.

"You raise your own kids Rosetta, and leave mine alone. Stop trying to take my kids," Mama said.

"You think I don't know how you've been beating her with sticks and extension cords? She's just a child. You make her sleep out in the cold barn, and don't feed her or take care of her the right way!" Aunt Rosetta yelled out so the whole community could hear.

"Do you think I'm stupid Rosetta? I do no such thing to my children," Mama said.

"You mean you don't do it to Vanessa. You are going to burn in hell Janice, for mistreating one of God's children. My brother loved that child and you're trying to destroy her. What kind of mother are you?" she asked.

"I'm a good mother to my children. I discipline my kids. Is that a crime Rosetta?" Mama asked.

"It's a crime when you beat your child until she can't move," Aunt Rosetta said with an evil look on her face.

People began to stop and look at us. Mama picked me up off the ground and began dragging me towards the car. I began yelling and screaming for Aunt Rosetta to help me.

"Aunt Rosetta, help me. She is going to hurt me. Help me. Help me!" I screamed louder.

"Janice, please don't take her," my aunt cried while running up to the car.

"Help me Aunt Rosetta. Help me. Please," I begged some more.

My Uncle James was sitting in the driver's seat waiting for us to get in the car. He just looked straight ahead like nothing was going on. We got into the back seat of the car. Mama was holding me very tight, but I kept fighting her.

"James, don't drive off. You know this is wrong. James, look at me," Aunt Rosetta stated.

Uncle James just put the car in drive and drove off. I stood up on the back seat of the car yelling and screaming for Aunt Rosetta. That was the last day I saw her. Mama kept me locked away like an animal. Neither Aunt Rosetta nor any of my father's relatives were allowed on our property. Mama put up *No Trespassing* signs everywhere. She was very serious. She didn't want any of them to come see us; especially me.

As the song ended, I snapped back to reality. I drove on down the street with the pitiful memory of that day. It's sad when a mother is in competition against her daughter to win her husband's love. There is a big difference in the two. The love a father feels for his daughter is not the same as a husband loving his wife. I didn't understand why my mama couldn't get that through her thick head.

So many memories about that day filled my head as I drove from Vegas to Mississippi. It seemed like I had a bad childhood, but everything wasn't bad. It was during my childhood that I found Nikki to love me and protect me. It's true that's she's evil at times, but she makes me feel safe. Unlike other people, she's always by my side.

I began to think about the first time Nikki appeared in my life. I think I was about six years old at the time. That was when I fell off my horse and got a small fracture on my lower leg. Farrow had thrown me onto a rock. My father said he was surprised I didn't break my leg in two. I had to be in my room for a good two months, if I recall correctly. It was so boring, and Vanessa thought she was too cute to play with me. As I lay in my bed, this small voice began talking to me, so I decided to talk back. She looked just like me, and we played with each other for about two days. On the third day, my father came into the room and asked, "Who are you chatting with, baby girl?"

"Nikki," I replied.

"Who's Nikki? I don't see anyone in here but you," he replied.

"Over there Father," I pointed but nobody was there in the corner.

He sat down on the bed with a puzzled look on the face. I guess he was trying to figure out what to say to me. "Baby girl, you know it's not nice to talk to yourself. People might think you're crazy," he finally said.

"Father, she is real. I talk to her. She must have gone out the window," I replied.

My father looked at the open window, sighed and said, "Maybe you're right."

"Father, you don't believe me?" I asked.

"Truthfully baby girl, no I don't believe you. You can't talk to yourself. It's not good on you. People will try to lock you up in a nut house and throw away the key," he spoke.

"Throw away the key?" I asked, looking scared.

"Yes, they put people in there and don't give a care about them. So, just remember it's not good to talk to yourself," he said.

"Father, I didn't talk to myself. Nikki was here. I guess she's gone home to her mother and father," I said.

"It's going to be alright baby girl. I will always be around to talk to you. That way you can listen to my jokes. Knock. Knock..." he said.

I answered, "Who's there?"

"Orange," he said.

"Orange who?" I asked.

"Orange you going to let me come in?" he joked as he tapped me on the nose.

We laughed and Father headed out the room. He looked down at me and then towards the window. He shook his head and walked out. I was disappointed, because he didn't believe that Nikki was real. From that day on, I didn't talk to Nikki again until

the day those boys raped me. She came back into my life and stood by my side. She has done so many things for me since then.

Who in their right mind is going to kill for another? I sure didn't have the guts to kill anybody. Everyone labeled me as being weak. I'm not weak, but afraid to branch out and talk to people. All my life I had been beaten for voicing my opinion to or around people. Maybe something happened to my mama in her childhood, and she just did it to me. Maybe her mother or father beat her. This behavior had to be something that was taught or that came from experience. In my childhood memories, there are none of my grandparents. My mama's hometown was in Pittsburgh, Pennsylvania. She moved to Newcastle, Washington with my father after they graduated from high school.

It really makes you think. No matter what color you are or what age group you are in, evil can come in different ways. My mama was the queen of evil. She is the reason why I am what I am today. She tried to break me down and kill my spirit, but my love for my father kept me alive. She wanted me to believe that my father didn't love me, but who was she fooling? My father always told me to remember how much he loved me. He told me up until the day God took him home.

I graduated from high school and moved on to college. I finally got my degree and became a small time lawyer. After all the bullshit she took me through, I was still standing. Most kids would have flipped out by now. I had to be tough growing up, and I did it. It's sad that my father wasn't here to see his little girl succeed, but the good thing was, Uncle Herman saw me graduate. He was Aunt Rosetta's husband. She wanted to see me graduate from college, but she was very sickly. I wanted to go by and see

her before I left Newcastle, but I didn't want to see her down like my father was.

Last year Aunt Rosetta died and I didn't attend her funeral, because Vanessa didn't tell me until a week after they had buried her. When I found out, I went to both her and my father's grave site. I sat there talking to them both like they weren't dead. I didn't want them to die, but it seemed like God was taking away all the people that really loved me.

I shook my head and snapped back to reality. I had to stop going down memory lane. It hurt me to think of those memories. I wanted to keep them alive, but then again I didn't.

Chapter 25

As I pulled back up at the farmhouse I rented in Iuka, Mississippi, I saw Cowboy. "Damn, what the fuck is he doing here?" I asked myself.

He was standing there with dark blue overalls on, with a white dirty looking shirt. His hair was all fuzzy and shit. He looked so fucking dirty.

"Hey baby girl, I see you are back. I thought you were coming in tonight?" he asked.

"I was, but I got an early start. Why are you here?" I asked.

"Cleaned the place for ya," he replied.

"Why? I didn't need you to clean up," I said.

"I thought maybe I could help you out. I was about to clean the cellar for you, but its locked," he stated.

"You stay out of that cellar Cowboy. I don't want you snooping around here!" I blasted.

"No snooping baby girl, just some country cleaning," he replied with this big ass country grin on his face.

I began to walk off from the car and he said, "Well, pop the trunk, so I can carry your bags to the house."

"No, leave it alone. I will do it myself later. You go home and come back tomorrow. I'm tired," I replied.

"Yes ma'am. You did drive a long way," he said.

"Yes I did. Now run along and stop being so nosey," I told him.

Cowboy walked over to his truck and got in like a scolded little child. His face had turned as red as fire. I stood there and watched him as he drove away like a bat out of hell. He was just a country boy that didn't have shit to do. As he got out of my sight, I popped the trunk to the car. Jeremy lay there passed out cold. I touched his neck to feel a pulse. He jumped, and looked up at me. I thought I heard something coming from the woods. I looked around trying to see where the noise came from. It was probably Cowboy snooping around peeping. I didn't know how I was going to get rid of that fool. If he kept this up, I would have to do away with him.

I grabbed my purse and closed the trunk back down. It wasn't safe to move Jeremy now. I needed to make sure that Cowboy was at home. I would give him a call later after I cleaned myself up.

After taking a bath and eating, I took a short nap. My body was tired and I didn't have the energy to lift Jeremy up out the car.

As I fell asleep one of my childhood memories invaded my space again. It was one of Vanessa and me playing with our dolls. She had a tea set and we pretended to have a tea party.

"Nicole, you and your doll can't have any tea," she said while snatching away the tea cup.

"Why not Vanessa?" I asked.

"Because Mama says you are evil. And evil people can't have tea at my party," she replied.

"I'm not evil Vanessa," I said.

She gathered up her stuff and pushed me out of her room. I stood there looking at her white wooden door, then put my head down and walked to my room. I sat on the bed, and held onto the small white poles of my bed, as I leaned my head against one. From where I sat, I could see Farrow running around in the open field. He was running wild, as free as a bird. I wished I was that free. Free of all this misery; the cursing out, the beatings, the pain and the hurt. I pretended like I was living somewhere else. I laid back on the bed and let my mind wander. How good it would feel to have a mother and father loving me, treating me like an angel.

Suddenly, my mama burst through the door, screaming at me. I jumped up off the bed and she grabbed me.

"Did you do this to Vanessa's doll?" she asked in a rude tone while shoving a doll with her eyes poked out into my face.

"No Mama," I replied.

"Well, Vanessa said you did it," she stated as she grabbed me by the shirt and began pulling me outside the house to the barn. She opened the big doors and pushed me inside.

"You stay in here until you learn to respect your sister's things," she said.

She closed the door on me. I stood there in the dark barn, then I gathered the small flashlight my father had given me and turned it on. I climbed up the small stairs to the loft, and stopped to look out at the house. Mama and Vanessa were seated at the kitchen table eating. I sat down on the edge, and looked at them two have fun. So many questions came to mind. Why won't they accept me? What did I do so wrong to deserve this?

After they finished eating, Vanessa washed the dishes and they disappeared into the back of the house. My flashlight was getting weaker and weaker. Finally, the light went out and I was stuck in the dark. I curled up next to a bale of hay in a corner. I could see flashes of lightning sparking throughout the sky. The thunder began to roar loud, and the rain began beating against the barn hard. I was scared out of my mind; I curled farther back into the corner and said, "Father, please help me."

I heard a dog bark, and I jumped up out of my sleep. My clothes were kind of wet from sweat; these nightmares were becoming so real. I rubbed my head. It seemed like I'd slept forever. I looked over at the clock, and it read two o'clock. Damn, I had slept for almost six hours.

"Nikki, you forgot about Jeremy. What are you doing?" Nicole asked.

"What about him? All you talk about lately is him," I said

"Nikki, you still have him locked away in the trunk of the car. He could be dead by now. You haven't given him any food or nothing to drink," Nicole replied.

"Damn," I said as I jumped up, grabbed the keys and ran to the car.

I popped the trunk, and he lay there staring. The inside light of the trunk had come on. I reached in and took the gray duct tape off of his mouth. He stretched his mouth open, and licked out his tongue. He began blinking his eyes, trying to focus, and started moving around trying to stretch himself out. I guess he was getting stiff from being in that position for so long. Then he would be tired, hungry, and thirsty. I continued to stare at him as tears began rolling down my face. My heart was becoming weak for him.

"I'm going to let him go," Nicole spoke as she grabbed the rope to untie Jeremy.

"Bitch, are you crazy? He's going to kill you the first chance he gets. Look in his eyes; you see nothing but fear," Nikki replied.

"I can't let you keep hurting him like this," Nicole said.

"Bitch, take your hands off the rope," Nikki demanded.

"Jeremy, I'm so sorry," Nicole stated as she placed a kiss on his forehead.

"Nicole. Focus. He's going to kill you bitch," Nikki stated.

"I am focused Nikki; I love him so much. You have to stop this," Nicole pleaded.

"Get your hands off the rope. I'm here to protect you. If you untie him, he will hurt you," Nikki said.

Nicole let go of the rope and stood back staring. She was beginning to get the control back. *I have to stop this bitch before she gets us killed,* Nikki thought to herself.

"Nicole, I know you're in there. Please help me," Jeremy spoke out.

"I want to, but Nikki will kill you if I do," she replied.

"Nicole, I love you so much. Please help me. Please help me," he said as he began to cry.

"What if she hurts you? I wouldn't be able to live with myself," Nicole said.

"If we work together, we both can take her. Please untie the ropes," Jeremy urged.

"Jeremy, I can't do it," Nicole said.

"Damn, Nicole. Help me," he begged.

Nicole fell back onto the ground and began crying out very loudly. She began rolling from side to side. Her clothes were getting dirty from laying on the dirt and rocks.

"God, please help me. What am I doing? I can't stop Nikki. Help me!" Nicole called out.

Nicole lay there crying and crying and crying until suddenly, she stopped bluntly. I wiped my tears away, and sat up on the ground. We couldn't keep fighting against each other. One of us had to go. I hated to kill Nikki, but she was becoming a pain in my ass.

"Bitch, you will never get rid of me. Try, and we all die," Nikki said as she got off the ground and looked down at Jeremy.

I snatched him by the ropes and began pulling him out of the car. As I got him on the edge of the trunk, I let his body go, and he fell to the ground abruptly. He let out a loud cry.

"Shut up," I yelled as I kicked him in the stomach. I asked, "Why are you turning Nicole against me? We have always been together as one. Do you think I'm going to let you come between us? Nicole is my world. My life."

"Nicole, I know you're in there. Baby, you can stop her," Jeremy pleaded while looking up at me.

"Didn't I say Nicole wasn't here bitch? I should take you out the game now, but I think I will save the best for last. You need to be tortured for using me; for fucking me, and throwing me away like dirty trash. For not wanting me, you fucking prick," I spat out.

"You fucking bitch! Go ahead and kill me! Kill me bitch!" Jeremy yelled out.

"Not now Jeremy; I have plans for you," I said

"Don't wait bitch; do it now. I can't take this anymore. Why are you doing this to me?" he asked.

"Why are you doing this to me?" I mocked him.

I grabbed the rope and began pulling him towards the cellar. "Damn bitch, you're heavier than I thought," I stated as I pulled harder and harder.

"Fuck you bitch; I'm going to kill your ass when I get loose," he said.

"You will never leave this farmhouse. Nobody comes out here. You can scream and shout all you want, but not a soul will hear you," I replied.

"Nicole, can you hear me? Nicole!" Jeremy yelled.

"Stop yelling for that bitch," I sneered.

"Nicole, please baby. Nicole, listen to me. I love you. I love you. I fucking love you so much," he stated as he began to cry again. I stopped at the front door of the cellar and sat down.

This feeling of remorse came over me, and Nicole was back. She got under Jeremy's head and held him in her lap. They began to cry together. Her salty tears fell in his face.

"Jeremy, I'm so sorry for letting Nikki do you like this. Please forgive me," Nicole apologized.

"Nicole, I love you. I've always loved you. Baby, you can help me. Stop Nikki," he sobbed.

"I can't; she will hurt you," Nicole replied.

"Just get me out of these ropes and I will save the both of us," he said.

"What about Nikki?" I asked.

"Fuck Nikki!" he yelled out.

Nicole became quiet and her face turned stone cold.

"Bitch, you can't control me. Never," I leaned down and whispered in his ear. I got off the ground and continued to drag him.

"Fuck you Jeremy. Nicole is mine forever. That bitch will always be weak," Nikki said.

"Leave her alone Nikki. Let her go," Jeremy said.

Before he could say anything else I began to drag his sorry ass down the old wooden steps of the cellar. He deserved to die. Leave it up to me; he would never hurt another woman again. Never.

Jeremy let out a loud cry. I tried to pull him, but his body wouldn't move. I looked to see what the problem was, and I saw that a sharp piece of wood had stuck into the lower part of his arm. He cried out like a little bitch. "I thought you were a man," I said as I loosened up the rope and pulled him harder down the steps. The sharp piece of wood broke off in his arm. Blood rolled down the wood and onto the floor and I dragged him on over to the bed. A blood trail followed us. I laid him on his stomach and walked back over to the steps. One of the steps was shredded.

I walked back over to Jeremy, turned him over on his side and said, "Well, I guess you want me to say I'm sorry."

"Fuck you Nikki," he spat.

"I know you want to. I will save that for later," I laughed.

I walked away from him and proceeded to a small medicine cabinet with all my goodies inside, that I had stocked before I left. I picked up one of my big needles with Ativan inside. I looked at the needle, and squirted some of the medicine out to make sure the syringe was working properly.

"Don't do it Nikki," Nicole pleaded.

"I have to untie him to hook him up. This will knock him out; not kill him," I said.

"That's too dangerous," Nicole said.

"Bitch, let me handle this. You run along and stop fucking with me before I do some real damage," I threatened.

I walked back over to Jeremy, raised the sleeve of his shirt and stuck him with the needle. He was out in seconds. I untied the ropes and his arms and legs fell slowly to the floor. As I undressed him and prepared him for bed, I thought I heard a noise outside. I ran up the wooden stairs and out the front cellar door. I looked out, but there was nothing to be seen. I had to hurry up because Cowboy was known to just pop up at my house without a warning.

I rushed back downstairs, undressed Jeremy and left nothing on but his boxers. I pulled back the purple and gray striped comforter on the bed, and lifted his body by his shoulders. I struggled and struggled until I finally got him on the bed. He was nothing but dead weight. After all the struggle, I tied him to the

bed with steel handcuffs and chains. There was no way he was getting away from me.

I looked at the stick pierced into his arm; I had to get it out. Since he was asleep, this would be a great time to do so. I gathered some rubbing alcohol, peroxide, and bandages. I pinned his arm back against his body and pulled on the wooden piece. His body gave a small jerk of some kind. I threw the wood on the floor and pushed a towel under his arm to stop the blood from getting on the bed. I poured the peroxide on the wound to get rid of the germs, and it fizzed up. Then I poured the rubbing alcohol onto it. His body starting jerking a little. I guess he could feel that even while being knocked out. After treating the wound, I bandaged him up.

After all that, I just stared at his body. I was trying to figure out why Nicole was so in love with this piece of shit. He was nothing but a low down dirty dog. He loved to use women. It was sad that he was going to have to die for all men that used women and treated them like shit. He didn't love them or care to be with them, but he would fuck them and leave them heart broken. Jeremy would think twice before he broke another woman's heart. Well, maybe not; because after this, he would die.

I scanned every inch of his body and my eyes landed on his cock. Even when he was soft, there was a print. I looked up at his face and he looked so sweet and innocent. I grabbed his cock softly through his pants, and stroked and stroked it. Finally, I pulled on the front of his boxers, and exposed his cock. It looked so fat and juicy. I fiddled around a little more, just stroking and stroking. I even bent down and began to suck him. After a few minutes, I stopped. I stood up and looked at it; I lightly hit it,

rocking it to one side. I lifted the boxers back up because there was nothing he could do for me now. *Absolutely nothing.*

As I looked at Jeremy laid out on the bed it reminded me of the first time my father had ever touched me. He was lying back on his bed when I walked in. I ran over to him, not thinking or knowing what he was doing to himself. He didn't flinch or anything when I jumped up on the bed and looked down at his dick. He was pulling and pulling at it. I guess at the time he was trying to get it hard. He had this funny look on his face and I was just smiling away. I asked him what he was doing and he said making himself happy. I didn't know what it meant, so I asked if I could make him happy too. Father took my hand and placed it on his dick. He began showing me how to stroke him. It didn't feel right, but I kept doing it. I asked if I could leave and go outside, and he told me no. We stroked and stroked until he was hard. After that day, father loved me like he did Mama. I didn't know any better at that time, but I wanted to make him happy. I snapped back to reality and looked into Jeremy's face. He was still out cold. Hopefully, he would have a long night's rest. I wanted to torture him and beat him until he decided he wanted to be with me and Nicole. Nicole was too weak for Jeremy. He needed a real woman; a woman who was willing to do anything in the world for him.

I thought about burning his body with candle wax until he screamed like a fucking girl or then again, burn him with cigarettes. All kinds of thoughts invaded my mind as I rubbed his legs. If he wasn't going to love me on his own, then I was going to make him do it.

"Nikki, I told you to leave him alone. Why do you keep messing with Jeremy? Remember, you said that you didn't want him," Nicole spoke.

"I don't want him, but I don't want you to have him either. He is too weak for you. The only person you need is me. I am here for you forever," I replied.

"I need a man in my life to love me, Nikki; not a woman," Nicole said.

"You're right. You've been fucked by women and men. How disgusting, but luckily I came along and tried to save you," I replied.

"How could you save me Nikki? Every time one of them molested me, you disappeared and didn't return until the next day. I needed you to protect me while they were there hurting me," Nicole said.

"I know Nicole. That's why I'm protecting you from any and everybody now. Nobody will ever hurt you again. I promise to protect you and give you the love you deserve," I told Nicole.

"I know you will Nikki. That's why I love you so much," Nicole said.

I walked back up the stairs and locked the cellar door. I sat down on the ground and cried. This was the man I loved, and I had him trapped like a caged animal. I didn't want him to feel how I had been feeling all these years, but it would all be over soon. He wouldn't live long to hurt like me.

Chapter 26

The next morning I lay in bed staring up at the ceiling. I was not feeling happy or sad. It seemed like my body was just there. I lay still until I heard something. It sounded like someone yelling out. "Damn, that's fucking Jeremy," I stated.

I jumped up, grabbed the keys, and headed to the cellar. After unlocking the door, I ran downstairs. He lay out on the bed helplessly.

"Bitch, where you been? I have to use the fucking bathroom," he said.

"Well, use it on yourself because I will never untie you," I answered.

"Are you fucking stupid? I'm not using the bathroom on myself. You have me fucked up. Now untie me," Jeremy demanded.

"You have to piss or shit?" I asked.

"What does it matter? Untie me, bitch," he repeated.

I ran back to the house to get my 9 mm. I would let him loose, but if he tried anything, I'd kill him. I ran back to the cellar

and said, "I'm going to untie one of your arms, but if you even flinch at me, I'm going to lay you dead where you stand."

"Just untie me," he said.

I pulled a bucket over to the left side of the bed for him to piss and do whatever he wanted to. I placed some tissue on the bed so he could reach it. As I unfastened the handcuff, I jumped back out the way toward the stairs. He jumped up off the bed and took out his cock to pee; he looked like he could barely stand. I moved to the bottom of the stairs, took a seat and watched him as he watched me. He turned around and sat down on the bucket to take a shit. After he finished, he wiped himself.

"Now lay your ass back down so I can handcuff you," I demanded as I pointed the gun toward him.

"I'm not going to try anything," he replied.

"I know you aren't going to. I'd hate to kill you," I said.

"Bitch, you ain't going to do shit. If that's the case, you would have killed me already," he taunted.

"Well, don't tempt me," I replied.

"You do realize that I haven't eaten or drunk anything? I guess you plan on starving me to death," he said.

"I might just do that. Now lay down and shut the fuck up," I ordered.

He did as I instructed him and I got the handcuff back on. I reached over to the table, put hand sanitizer on his hand, and

rubbed. He grabbed my hand gently. I looked at him and snatched my hand back.

"I'm going to bring you something to eat. Give me a few minutes," I said.

I walked out the cellar and locked the door behind me. Before I could reach the front door, Cowboy pulled up in his old beat up truck. I hid the gun behind my back.

"Howdy girl!" he yelled out the window.

"Hi Cowboy," I greeted.

"What you doing?" he asked.

"I'm about to get me something to eat and then go into town," I said.

"What you need in town? I can drop by the store and get it," he offered.

"That's okay; I need to get away from here anyway," I replied.

"Okay girl. Are you almost finished with my ride?" he asked.

"Not yet. I have to clean it up then give it back to you," I said.

"You don't have to do all that. I can do that for you," he replied.

"No Cowboy, I will clean it up. You gave it to me clean and I will give it back to you clean," I responded.

"Okay, that's on you," he stated as he drove off back down the dirt road. I watched as he disappeared. He was really beginning to work my nerves.

I walked back inside and cooked Jeremy some smoked bacon, Texas style biscuits, Jimmy Dean sausages and grits with lots of butter. Just the way he like it. Then I fixed him some homemade sweet tea, and took it all to him. I took the handcuff off his left arm and let him eat. He was right handed, so he had more strength in that one. He was eating like no tomorrow. In a way, I kind of felt bad for him.

After he finished eating, he asked for some more, so I fixed him some more food. He drank three glasses of tea and two glasses of water. Damn, I was really starving that nigga. He lay down on the bed and I handcuffed him back.

"Why are you doing all of this? You never told me why," he said.

"Do I really have to tell you why? Seriously, you don't know?" I asked.

"No. I don't know," he replied.

"I love you Jeremy; but you don't love me," I answered.

"Nicole, I do love you. Or are you Nikki right now?" he asked.

I didn't even answer. After we stared at each other for a few minutes, he finally dozed off. Maybe he was confused about who to love. Nicole loved him, not me; but I would love to see why she loved him so much. He had to have something special for her to want him; then again Nicole would love anyone who would love

her. Anyone who would show her some attention. I would let him sleep today, but tonight was our night. I was going to fuck Jeremy whether Nicole liked it or not. She didn't deserve to have all the fun. I wanted to have fun too.

Chapter 27

I dashed a bucket of water on Jeremy's face, and he jumped to wakefulness.

"What the fuck are you doing?" he asked.

"Wake your punk ass up. It's six o'clock in the evening and you are still sleep. We have to talk," I replied.

"About what? I want to talk to Nicole, not you," he said.

"Fuck Nicole. I will let you talk to her, but first I want to know why. Why do you like breaking women's hearts?" I asked.

"What?" he asked.

"Explain to me why you like using women?" I asked.

"You mean why did I use you? I didn't use you at all; I do love you," he replied.

"Stop lying Jeremy, you don't love me," I said.

"You're right. I don't love you Nikki; but I love Nicole. Can I please talk with Nicole?" he asked.

"Why? Because she's weak and wants to love you? I'm here to protect her. To make sure you don't fuck with her head again," I responded.

"Please Nikki, let me talk to Nicole," he repeated.

I sat there on the bed and just looked at him. My hands began to rub the calf of his leg, then moved up toward his thighs. He let out a low sigh as if he was enjoying it. I jumped up on the bed and began kissing his thighs. I rubbed my tongue all over him. I saw his cock rising through his boxers, and I rubbed my head back and forward, teasing it. Jeremy began to squirm.

"Oh Nicole, this feels so good," he whispered.

I looked up at him and he stared back. I pulled down his boxers, and exposed his hard cock. My mouth found its way to the head and licked. Before I knew it; I was sucking and sucking him hard, like a vacuum cleaner. You could hear nothing but me slurping and licking his cock and balls.

"Oh shit, this feels so good," Jeremy slowly said.

After I sucked him, and he didn't cum, I had no choice but to fuck him. I figured if I continued, he would release. I got up off the bed, undressed myself and climbed back onto the bed. I straddled his hard cock and slowly moved down. He penetrated me like he wanted me. The chains and handcuffs began to rattle as he moved his arms. As I stroked him, he stroked me back. We were stroking and stroking until he came all in my pussy. I lifted myself, and the cum rolled out of my pussy and down his cock in clots. I got off him, and began to suck him again and again, taking him and waiting for him to get hard for a second time; but his cock wouldn't get hard again.

"What's wrong? Why aren't you hard again?" I asked.

"Because I'm finished. I can't perform again," he replied.

"You will fuck me again," I demanded.

"I want to make love to Nicole. You aren't Nicole," he said.

"You bitch. I want to fuck again!" I yelled as I got off the bed.

Jeremy just leaned his head to the opposite side of me. He began to shake his head from side to side.

"Why are you doing this to me?" he asked.

"Are you fucking serious? You used me, and you won't use another woman again," I said.

"How? Please explain to me how?" He asked.

"You fucked me and just left me like I was nothing. You didn't care for me; only about what I could give you. I fucked you whenever. I sucked your cock whenever, and let you fuck me in my ass whenever you felt like it. But you didn't give a fuck. I cooked for you and did so much to please," I ranted.

"I didn't fucking ask you to!" he yelled.

"Bitch, you don't have to ask when you love someone. I loved you so much!" I yelled back.

"Nicole baby, that's you?" he asked.

"Yes Jeremy, it's me. I loved you and you never loved me back," I said.

"Nicole baby, I do love you. Please, let's just go away—me and you. I want you to be my wife. Let's get married," he stated while trying to sit up.

"What about Nicole?" I asked.

"We can take her too. Please baby, let's get away from here," he said.

Jeremy stopped and realized what he said. "You mean we can take Nikki?" he asked.

"No bitch; Nicole is not here. You are nothing but a dog. You want to fuck both of us. You want me and her," I stated while walking towards the wooden stairs.

"Bitch, you tricked me. You tricked me!" he yelled out while I walked up the stairs.

"Nicole please! Nicole! Nicole please don't leave me," Jeremy kept repeating over and over until I slammed the cellar doors. I walked inside the house and lay on the bed.

"I told you he is mine Nikki. Why are you trying to take him away from me?" Nicole said.

"Bitch, I wanted to see why you are so in love with this nigga. He is no good, and you still want to be with him. That's fucking stupid," I replied.

"Nikki, don't call me stupid. I love him and I will do anything to protect him," Nicole said.

"Yes I see. But can you protect him from me? I will take him out if you keep interfering with me. You are really getting on my last fucking nerve. I've had enough of you," Nikki stated clearly.

Chapter 28

My heart had a deep cut within. Jeremy wanted me and Nicole. How could he not want just me? Nicole was weak and a burden, and we would never survive with her on our team. I didn't want him at first, but now I do. He had fucked me and I liked it. I could finally see why Nicole was so crazy for him.

"Nikki, I can hear you. You leave Jeremy alone. He is mine," Nicole said.

"Bitch, I want him. There is no way I'm going to let you have him now. Did you see us making love to each other?" I goaded while getting up off the bed and dancing around the room.

"You tricked him. You deceived him. He will never want anyone like you," Nicole said.

"We will see bitch. We will see," I replied.

"You're just like Mama and Vanessa. You aren't here to protect me. Why you trying to hurt me?" Nicole asked while whining.

"How dare you compare me to those bitches? I've always been on your team. Always," I said.

"What about now Nikki? You want Jeremy and you know I love him," Nicole said.

"You just being a greedy bitch Nicole," I said.

Nicole began whimpering like a fucking baby so I lay on the bed, curled up like a baby, and went to sleep. I needed to take a short nap before our journey tonight. Tonight was the night I would kill Nicole and Jeremy. If he didn't want me, so be it. Nicole wanted him, but would never have him. I wouldn't let that pussy ass female have him. Never.

I woke up because I kept hearing noises. I looked over at the clock, and it said eleven thirty. Damn, I'd slept too late. I sat up on the bed, and listened more closely. My head began beating like someone hitting a drum. I held my head with both hands, trying to make it stop. I looked up at the walls, and they seemed to be swaying from side to side. Nicole's voice was letting out a loud cry that stung my ears. Voices and more voices began to invade my mind. Everyone I killed, I could see their faces on the wall staring at me.

"What you looking at?" I yelled while holding my head. They all began to laugh out loud while pointing at me. I was shaking my head violently, trying to stop all the madness.

"Nikki, you need to get a grip. What's going on with you Nikki?" Nicole asked.

"What are you doing to me? We are supposed to be a team. Together as one," I said.

"I'm not doing anything. That's you. You're losing it, and you said I would be the one to get us busted," Nicole said.

"Shut up bitch," I stated as the images on the wall disappeared.

Finally, my head stopped beating, and the voices disappeared. I looked at the wall, trying to focus, but there was nothing there. As I got myself together, I heard the noise again. It sounded like it was coming from the cellar. I put on my shoes and headed out the door. I looked at the cellar doors as I ran up to them, and noticed they were wide open. I ran back to the house to get the 9 mm. I didn't want to be unprotected and have him kill me. As I ran out the front door again, I began throwing up everywhere. My head began spinning, and it seemed like the cellar doors were moving back and forth. This couldn't be happening to me now. I stood still for a few seconds, and focused on the door. I got myself together, ran down the stairs, and saw Jeremy standing there. He was unshackled; no chains, and no handcuffs. He stared at me as I looked at him. It seemed like we were both frozen. I lifted the gun and released one round into his shoulder. Before I could shoot again, I looked up into this picture on the wall and saw a reflection of Cowboy. Before I could turn around and shoot him, he hit me in the back of the head, knocking me unconscious. *Bitch.......*

PUBLICATIONS
PRESENTS...

Get ready to go on the ride of your life with Felix and his 4 women of choice. Nikki, Rhonda, Meka, and Toya each have a thing for Felix that they cannot describe. It's not only because he is the youngest and most sought after attorney in Washington, D or the fact that he is handling a high profile multi-million dollar divorce case, but that he serves them real well! Felix makes it happen with each woman like they are each his woman, and that just what they expect from him...A monogamous relationship which is what they each think they are getting. What will happen when jealousy, lies, deceit, millions of dollars, paternity, and feelings become at risk? Is 4play enough to make Felix fall in love? Do you think Felix will keep getting over or will the women get even? Ride the roller coaster as he vows to never fall in love but is enjoying the "loving" from 4 women from 4 different walks of life. You will definitely be able to relate to one of these women if not all! Laugh, cry, and enjoy Felix's lavish lifestyle of 4play!!!!

The Wrong He's Done
A Novel by
Nathan Gadsden

Greatness is only a step away for Damon Masters. Partnership at his firm is within his grasp; all Damon has to do is prove to the firm that he can handle its main client. His wife, Priscilla, has found entreprenuerial success at her boutiques. The only speed bump in life is his annoying mother-in-law, Queen, whose jealous ways wreak havoc on his marriage. When the firms client turns out to be Frank Vanetti, mob boss and racketeer, Damon has to decide whether his life is worth risking for the idea of greatness. In the meantime, Queen has managed to split his household, leaving him to pick up the pieces of his fractured marriage. With the help of his best friend, Antoine, Damon goes on a road trip to meet past loves and reevaluate where life went wrong. But walking away from Vanetti does not mean that Damon is safe from the mob. And best friend Antoine's schemes and manipulations seek to sabotage Damon's trip and further destroy what is left of his marriage. When ex-loves remind Damon of what he had, and all the drama and chaos of his current life become overwhelming, he must decide whether his current life is worth fighting for.

NOW AVAILABLE

Daughter of the Gar

"This may sound like your typ
street-lit novel but it is anyth
but... this is one of those boo
that will have you on the edge
your seat, trying to figure
where the story is going. Daugh
of the Game is chock full of li
deceit, betrayal, and murder. I w
hard pressed to put this no
down...that is just how good t
book is. I was drawn to the sto
and the characters right from t
start. I absolutely loved this bo
and eagerly anticipate t
seque

–Leona, APOOO Book Cl

In Daughter of the Game, The game devours life and life devour
love. It's obvious that Armand is a hustler on the rise. As long as
he keeps that life separate from Monique, she is willing to be his
everything. Needing Armand's love, she hides her true identity.
Armand has no clue that Monique's father is the ruler of all vice,
so deep in the game that most hustlers work for and answer to
him without ever knowing it. In a moment of weakness, Armand
submerges Monique into his underworld, exposing her to his
secrets and risking her life to his enemy. When that enemy turns
out to be her father, Monique finds herself in a cruel tango
between family loyalty and all consuming love. Can true love
outlast the game? Or must love be sacrificed for both of them to
survive?

NOW AVAILABLE

KAI

The Loudest Silence

All night? With his best friend? Then wants the fruit to be juicy when he climbs into bed? Would you believe the obvious, that there was something going on, or continue to turn your head since he was the prince charming that saved you from the ghetto? Do you get even for what you know, must be happening, as he whispers to her every night?

What would happen if you glanced in your home window and saw your wife making passionate love to your best friend's husband. Would you point the gun at him or her?

Gaps of inexplicable time lead to drastic assumptions, jail, and even death as the silence is so loud that it could destroy all four lives...

When Silence is the only answer given and the timing is never right, nothing is what it seems nor will it ever be the same again!

NOW AVAILABLE

Publications Presents

The hottest stripper in the DMV, Fancy, is on a mission. Whil[e] everyone else see's her as a money hungry hoe, she laughs a[s] they have no idea what she is thirsty for...BLOOD. Fancy ha[s] protected her baby sister Liv all her life and now its time to punish those who caused her to grow up too fast.

Liv lives in her cushy bubble that her big sister Fancy has created for her over the years but she has her secrets as wel[l]

She has secretly been accepting money from her "father" throughout the last couple of months, but she was told that he[r] father died.

When lies come to light, Fancy and Liv have to decide where their loyalty lies and who has really been Deceitfully Wicked.

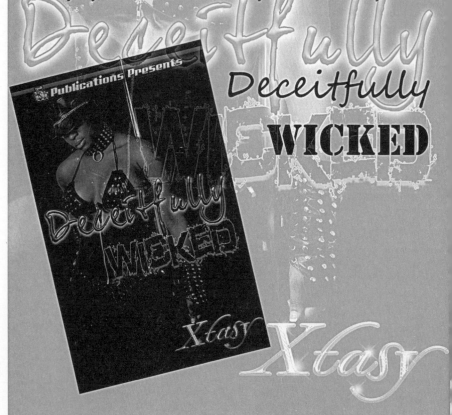

Deceitfully

WICKED

Xtasy

Publications Presents...
Wanting
Crazy
A Sexy Novel by
V. Yates

COMING 2011

5 STAR PUBLICATION

www.icon5star.com

info@icon5star.com

301.568.2588

If you are an aspiring author, or already an author looking for a publishing company you can call home and be a part of the family, 5 Star Publications is now accepting manuscripts from authors of all levels!!

If you or someone you know are an author and looking for a bookstore to support your work of art look no further, TLJ Bookstore is the answer!

TLJ BOOKSTORE

www.tljbookstore.com

info@theliteraryjoint.com

301.420.1380

The Centre at Forestville

3383 Donnell Drive

Forestville, MD 20747